SECOND CHANCE

SECOND CHANCE

(Griffin Force #5)

JULIE COULTER BELLON

STONE
HALL
BOOKS

OTHER BOOKS BY JULIE COULTER BELLON

Canadian Spies Series

Through Love's Trials

On the Edge

Time Will Tell

Doctors and Dangers Series

All's Fair

Dangerous Connections

Ribbon of Darkness

Hostage Negotiation Series

All Fall Down (Hostage Negotiation #1)

Falling Slowly (Hostage Negotiation #1.5)

Ashes Ashes (Hostage Negotiation #2)

From the Ashes (Hostage Negotiation #2.5)

Pocket Full of Posies (Hostage Negotiation #3)

Forget Me Not (Hostage Negotiation #3.5)

Ring Around the Rosie (Hostage Negotiation #4)

Griffin Force Series

The Captive

The Captain

The Captain's Christmas Promise

The Capture

Second Look

Second Chance

Lincoln Love Stories

Love's Broken Road

Love's Journey Home

Veteran Club Regency Series

The Marquess Meets His Match

The Viscount's Vow

The Highlander's Hidden Heart

Cover Design by Steven Novak Illustrations

Copyright © 2021

ISBN-13- 978-1-7363129-1-9

Printed in the United States of America

First Printing February 2021

10 9 8 7 6 5 4 3 2 1

ACKNOWLEDGMENTS

I am so grateful to the people around me who help me do what I love and make all my books shine.

I have to thank Jon and Jeni, my amazing beta readers who catch all my big picture mistakes and editing errors and make me look good. I hope you know how much I value both of you!

My critique partner, Annette, who is so encouraging and supportive. She's a fantastic cheering squad of one for me, right when I need it most. Thank you for that, Annette!

And a huge thank you to the Griffin Force series fans who are always asking me for the next story, I love you guys! Thanks for caring about these characters.

My family, especially my husband, are the most important people in my life and I am forever grateful that they are always willing to step up when I have a deadline and help me make it work. I love you!

For Brandon. You inspire me every day with your courage and kindness.

CHAPTER ONE

Augie Taylor had criss-crossed the world with Griffin Force chasing terrorists, but this would be his first time in Libya---well, it would be if they actually made it out of Libyan airspace and onto Libyan soil.

He peered out of the tiny airplane window, but he couldn't see much. A few flares were the only light on the ground to guide the pilot of their six-seater plane. There appeared to be some sort of struggle between the pilot and the elements, though, since the plane was catching air and getting farther away from the lights instead of closer to them. Were they going to overshoot the landing zone? His stomach twisted into knots, and he thought he might throw up. *Don't think about it.*

He took a deep breath and tried reciting Abel's Binomial theorem to himself. Anything to distract him from thinking about the statistic that almost half of fatal crashes happened on final descent or landing.

Nate reached across the aisle and patted him on the arm. "Try to relax."

Augie gave him a smile, hoping it didn't look as weak as he felt. The plane bobbed a bit more, and Augie gripped his armrests. "Abby, what did you say your contact's name was?" Maybe if he concentrated on the reason he was going to Libya, he could take his mind off of the nausea roiling through him.

She glanced back, her eyes full of sympathy. "Malek. He's meeting us as soon as we land. We'll be at the safe house in no time." The plane took a final lurch before it touched down and rumbled over the uneven ground of the field. "See? We made it," Abby said, grinning over at him.

Augie took a breath. "Sure did." When the plane finally stopped, he nearly jumped from his seat. Grabbing his laptop bag from the floor, he straightened. The doors weren't open yet, but standing in a stationary plane felt much better. Colt's arms were raised as he stretched in the seats near the front. He hadn't noticed Augie's distress. That was the only good thing about sitting near the back. He didn't want Colt to think there were situations he couldn't handle in the field.

Colt, Abby, and Nate were first to exit the plane. They all quickly walked to the front and helped offload their bags and equipment. When they were finished, the group moved back as the pilot readied to take off again. Augie watched him go, the plane climbing higher into the sky before disappearing into the night. They were safely on the ground. Sort of. How safe was anyone in Libya, really?

The others had already begun walking toward the van that shone its headlights at the edge of the field. Augie caught up and kept pace with Abby. "I've been monitoring all the usual channels, but so far no new chatter on Atwah."

"I think we would have heard whispers if he'd left Libya," she said. "But my contact will have the latest."

They walked toward the man who leaned against the hood of a small van, his arms folded. Dents marred the van's front bumper and, if Augie had to guess, it hadn't been washed in at least a year. There was barely enough clean space for the driver to see out of the windshield. But it was hard to tell anything more when there were only headlights, the moon, and dying flares penetrating the darkness.

Abby held out her hand. "Malek, it's been too long."

He took her hand and bowed over it slightly. "We have much to discuss, but we can't linger here. Let's get you to the safehouse."

She nodded, and Nate opened the van's sliding door. It was then that Augie noticed the driver, a young man wearing a long white shirt and vest, as well as a keffiyeh. He met Augie's eyes for just a moment before he looked away. Augie got into the van and sat down on a stained and torn seat right behind the driver. The faint smell of old gunpowder filled his nose. This van had seen some action at one time or another. Juggling his laptop bag on his lap, he made sure everything was secure and shut the door.

Malek and the driver spoke quietly to each other in Arabic before the van started up and got moving. The driver's voice had an odd timbre, like he'd been caught between puberty and manhood. Not low, but not high, either. He kept glancing at Abby, too. What was that about? Augie watched the back of the driver's head, wishing he had a view of the guy's face. Maybe he should run a background check on him. Abby knew Malek, but how much did she know about the driver?

Filing that on his mental to-do list, Augie turned to watch the shadowy scenery flashing past him. They'd made it to a paved road with soft edges broken by a few trees. It didn't take long until they were passing storefronts, most that were little more than a shell with a wall or two surrounded by rubble.

"Are we in Benghazi?" Augie asked, leaning forward.

Malek turned slightly. "Yes. I have a safehouse here that gets electricity several times a day. And I've rigged up an old satellite dish and a generator in such a way that we can get some reliable internet."

Augie had been told of the outages and spotty internet, but had hoped his intel was wrong. He was used to having the internet at his fingertips anytime he needed it on an op, but this one was going to be old school. They'd all have to rely on their field skills more than ever.

The driver pulled up in front of a small unit that looked like a gated garage. Houses on either side of it looked deserted and had several large gouge marks, as if the buildings had survived small mortar fire.

"Here we are," the driver announced, turning to look at Abby once more. She nodded and opened the door on her side. Augie did the same and waited for Colt and Nate to get out as well.

Malek led the way up the small walk and unlocked the gate. He seemed in a hurry to get inside and ushered them all through the front door before walking inside himself and turning on the light. They were in a small living room with three large wooden chairs and a worn sofa against one wall. The driver sauntered to the window and pulled back the heavy curtain slightly to look out. Was he making sure no one saw them?

"It's not much, but it will have to do." Malek shrugged and turned to Abby. "I know you're probably tired, and since there's only a few hours until sunrise, I'll come back once you've rested a bit and we can discuss why you're here."

Augie was listening to what was being said, but he was more focused on the driver. He'd come away from the window and arranged it so he was in the corner with a good vantage point for watching everyone, yet in the shadows where he might not be noticed. He was acting so strangely, it made Augie suspicious. He walked over and stood near him, trying to get a read on what he might be after. Could he be trusted? Should Augie say anything to Colt?

Abby shifted closer to Malek. "Thank you. For the safehouse and for getting us into the country. This mission is time-sensitive and with all the military checkpoints and curfews across Libya, we couldn't have gotten here in time without your help." Abby looked at Colt. "Before you go, I'd like to introduce you to Captain Colt Mitchell. He's the head of Griffin Force."

Malek nodded toward Colt, but quickly returned his gaze to Abby. "I'm sorry to be so blunt, but this is a very delicate time for our country. We have the opportunity to build a peace accord between General Saleh and Prime Minister al-Masli. Having foreign operations going on while we prepare is very dangerous. For you *and* us. I need to know what you plan to do in Libya." He flicked his glance to Colt. "Tomorrow. And then you can leave as quickly and quietly as you came."

Colt walked over to stand in front of Malek. "I understand what you're saying. And I support the peace talks. But we have reason to believe Atwah is in Libya. If that's true, Atwah will do all he can to destroy any steps toward peace."

Malek immediately shook his head. "No. Atwah is not here. General Saleh would have been informed."

"Maybe he was informed, but didn't choose to loop you in." Colt glanced at Abby before returning his gaze to Malek. "How close are you to the general?"

"I'm one of his advisors." Malek rubbed a hand over his face. He lifted a hand and motioned to the driver. "And by way of my own introductions, this is Rian Dahmani. He's a runner for the Libyan National Armed Forces, but moonlights for anyone who can pay. Not much happens in Benghazi without Rian knowing about it."

Rian bowed as well. "I'm happy to help with whatever you need while you're in Benghazi."

Augie was fascinated by the man's accent and couldn't hold back his curiosity any longer. "Where are you from?" he asked, trying to keep his tone casual. "I can't place your accent."

The driver glanced at him, but didn't answer. Abby stood and put her hand on Augie's shoulder. "I think we're all tired. Before we break for the night, can you go see what kind of internet connection we can expect? The sooner we get our communications set up, the better."

Augie frowned. Something was going on with the driver. He didn't know what it was, but he was determined to find out. He'd let it go for now, though.

"Okay," he said. He walked back the twenty paces to grab the duffel bag that held all their electronic equipment. "Which room is the best place to set up in?" He looked at Malek.

"The back bedroom is closest to the satellite dish." Malek glanced at Rian. "Go with him and show him the way. Then we'll head out."

Rian obeyed, walking past Augie and continuing on down the hall. He was wearing the traditional long white shirt and baggy pants and moved quickly, like a cat. Augie quickened his step, adjusting his hold on the duffel.

The back bedroom was a small square room with two barracks-style cots, a chest of drawers with one drawer missing, and a wooden table near a window. The window was covered with a heavy blanket, making the gray walls seem even more shadowy. Rian showed him where the electrical outlets were located and how to connect to the system they'd jerry-rigged to get internet. It didn't take Augie long to have everything set up.

"How did you figure out how to get internet service that wasn't state-controlled?" Augie kept his voice casual. He wanted to know more about this driver so he'd have something to go on when he did a background check.

"Malek is very talented in that area." Rian stood back a step to look at the table where the monitors and laptops were all buzzing to life. "Looks like you know what you're doing as well."

"How did you meet Malek?" Augie did a few checks of the bandwidth and strength of signal. Everything looked great, considering the position they were in of not having the normal infrastructure in place for reliable internet.

"We've both been involved with the resistance from the beginning." Rian started to move toward the door, but Augie stepped in front of him.

"You look a little young to have been part of the resistance for the last decade." Augie waited until Rian met his eyes. "Were you recruited to the cause or coerced?"

Rian's jaw clenched and he glared up at him. "Do you think to rescue me? You know nothing of what is going on in my country or what we need." He pulled away and stalked to the door. "You would do well to keep your opinions to yourself."

"Is that a threat?" Augie met him at the door, anger bubbling in his chest. "Who are you, really? Because I think you're hiding something."

If Augie hadn't been so close, he wouldn't have noticed Rian's quick intake of breath, as if his words had hit a nerve. Rian recovered quickly, though, and lifted his chin. "Be very careful. One whisper from me into the right ears and you might find yourself in a situation you and your men won't like." His words were soft, yet deadly.

Augie leaned in, using the two inches of height advantage he had. "Should we talk to Malek or Abby about that? Do they know how easy you would find it to betray us?"

"What's going on here?" Colt's voice cut the tension that had built between them. Augie stepped back. He clenched his fists and kept an eye on Rian. He knew the guy was hiding something. His body language was screaming it. But he had to be careful.

"Nothing's going on. I was just getting to know Rian better." Augie lifted his brows, daring Rian to contradict him.

Rian said nothing and pushed past Colt, heading back to the living room.

Colt watched him go, then stood in front of Augie. "That didn't look like nothing."

Augie waved a hand. "Something's off with that kid. He's hiding something, and I'm going to find out what it is."

Colt rubbed his chin. "You think we can't trust him?"

"That's exactly what I think." Augie glanced at the door, then lowered his voice. "He said that one whisper from him could put us in a situation we wouldn't like."

Quirking an eyebrow, Colt moved past Augie and put his duffel on a cot. "What brought that on?"

"I asked if he was recruited to the cause or coerced." Augie held up a hand. "I just want a little more information on this guy so I can do a background check."

"I've never seen you react so strongly to anyone." He furrowed his brows. "We'll keep an eye on him, and I'll mention your concerns to Abby. Maybe Malek could give us some background on the kid."

Augie nodded. "We did manage to get our communications set up. And there's a small generator in the house that we can use in case of an emergency and the electricity is out."

"That's good to know." Colt walked back to the door. "We've got a lot of work to do on this op if we're going to capture Atwah."

The sick feeling Augie had been fighting on the plane returned. They needed everyone on deck and all the skill and luck they could muster if they were going to catch Atwah. And they didn't need a driver with no loyalty to ruin all of that.

Augie couldn't let that happen. He was going to be watching Rian carefully. The kid wouldn't have the chance to betray them if Augie had anything to say about it. And that was a promise.

CHAPTER TWO

R ian picked her way through the burned-out building, careful to be as quiet as possible. The moon was hidden by the clouds, making this late-night meeting that much more eerie. But Khattalah was a trusted source and if she was going to verify that Atwah was in country, he would be the person to ask.

As she climbed over some large concrete pieces in the middle of the floor, Rian couldn't stop thinking about her confrontation at the safehouse with Augie. She hadn't been prepared for someone to question her so closely. In all her years of dressing as a young man, no one had zeroed in on her so quickly, and she hadn't known how to react. And by threatening him, she'd given Augie even more to be suspicious about. If she could have taken back her words last night, she would have. Malek trusted Griffin Force enough to help them get into Libya and hide them, and she trusted Malek. What had she been thinking to antagonize the computer tech? Now she would have to be extra careful not to draw any more attention to herself or give Augie any reason to think she would betray them.

She made it to the far west corner of the building where the stone wall of the broken building provided a little shadowy overhang near an exit. That's where Khattalah preferred to meet. When she got closer, she saw him leaning against the wall. He was dressed all in black except for a bright blue vest. He loved his colorful vests and had even shown her the shop where he bought them. He straightened when he saw her.

Cautiously moving toward him, she bowed slightly. *"As salam aleykum."*

Khattalah greeted her, his small eyes nervously sweeping the room behind them. "Things are dangerous just now," he said, his voice hardly more than a loud whisper. "With the peace talks so close, the Prime Minister, the General, and the foreigners have eyes everywhere. Every side looks for a reason to lock up anyone that they consider a traitor." He ran his sleeve over his forehead and looked around once more. Khattalah was sweating, but was it from the humidity or his anxiety? He was acting strangely.

"Let's be quick," Rian said, his nervousness triggering her own. She glanced around, but the building seemed as deserted as it had been when she arrived. "I've heard whisperings that Atwah might be coming to Benghazi. Have you heard anything like that?" Of course, she'd heard Atwah was already here, but Khattalah didn't need to know every detail.

Khattalah's dark eyes glittered in the muted moonlight that had managed to come through the broken window beside them. "Some men arrived at the training camp three days ago and one of them was immediately taken to a bunker. He is guarded 24/7 and no one has any idea who it is. I assumed it was a political prisoner, but perhaps they could be guarding Atwah?" He shook his head. "But what would Atwah want here? The legendary 'Ghost' who escaped from The Great Satan and her allies would not come to Libya."

Rian had no answer. If the man Khattalah described was Atwah, his presence could mean the end of the peace talks. A known terrorist being protected at the General's training ground would give the Prime Minister a reason to call everything off. All the efforts to bring peace to their country would be in vain.

"Can you bribe someone to find out who is in the bunker?" Rian shifted slightly so she was facing Khattalah straight on. "I'm sure there are others who would be willing to pay to know his identity so we could sell the information and recoup any costs."

Khattalah was already shaking his head. "Those who guard him bring him supplies. No one else is allowed in or out. I'm sure they could not be bought."

"Everyone has their price, but we couldn't pay more than our standard fee for information up front." She let out a breath, trying to think the situation through. "Perhaps this mysterious visitor isn't Atwah."

"Of course. But if it is Atwah, the General must be informed. I'm sure he would handsomely reward the bringer of such good news." Khattalah's lips curved into a smile as if he were imagining the General's praise.

"The bringer of such good news would be a laughingstock if it turns out that it was not Atwah after all, but a lowly courier for the Prime Minister or some such." Rian moved toward the exit, keeping her keffiyeh draped around her neck and chin. There wasn't any more to say, and it was time to go. She'd learned long ago that those who kept moving were the ones who stayed alive. "I'll be in contact."

Khattalah bowed slightly. "As will I."

But they both knew the race was on. Both of them would be trying to find out the identity of the man squirreled away at the training camp, and neither would be telling the other what they found. Khattalah was always looking out for himself, anything for a bit of money, recognition, or even food, but everyone with a shred of information had the same mindset. The country had been at war for so long it was hard to remember any other way of life.

She watched him leave before she went the opposite direction to the back of the building. She'd learned long ago to have several exit plans and never leave the same way she'd arrived.

She slipped out and headed toward the more inhabited part of town. Though there wasn't anyone visible on the streets, Rian could feel eyes on her. No one made a move in Benghazi without someone knowing about it. And with her secret, she had to be extremely careful that she wasn't caught unaware. She straightened her head covering and tried to shrink back into the shadows as much as she could.

When she passed the street that would take her to the safehouse where Malek had stashed Griffin Force, she was tempted to go back to see if Malek was still there. Likely, he'd gone back to the apartment building they were living in with several other men and boys loyal to General Saleh. It was like their little oasis in the middle of the bombed-out city. Only one side of the apartment building had been hit, the rest of it had livable space. Malek and others loyal to the cause had claimed it last year, and it had been nice to have a roof over her head that felt safe. For the time being.

Though she took a roundabout way and kept to the alleys and side streets, it wasn't very long before she was home. Pushing open the door to the lobby, the squeak sounded loud in the stillness of the night. Wincing, she hurried down the darkened hallway to her apartment. A few lights flickered overhead and she was anxious to get home. Stopping in front of her door, she unlocked it and stepped inside. Turning the lock behind her, she leaned against the door with a sigh. She'd made it. After a moment, she reached over to turn on the lights. A movement in the corner caught her eye and she whipped out her knife, pointing it at the intruder.

Malek held up his hands, but his face was impassive as if he'd been through this scenario hundreds of times. He probably had with how long he'd been fighting the war in Libya "It's me. I just wanted to know how things went with Khattalah. Did he know anything?"

Rian slowly put her knife away, willing her heart to slow. Ever since her confrontation with Augie, she'd been more jumpy than usual. "I did get a bit of information, but you won't like it."

She turned to the small refrigerator and took out two bottles of water. Walking into the living room, she handed one to Malek. "Someone important came to the training camp three days ago, but no one knows who. They've been in a bunker with two guards attending to them." She opened her water and took a long pull.

"That sounds like a prisoner, not someone of Atwah's importance." Malek twisted the lid of his water bottle but didn't open it.

"It fits with the timeline that Griffin Force gave us." Rian sat down in the wooden chair to her right. "But why would Atwah come here to hide? He has safehouses all over the world with better security."

"Exactly. If it is Atwah, he will have an agenda, and one that won't be good for Libya." Malek put the water bottle to his lips and drank it all in one gulp, then crushed the bottle. "We can't have any interference with the peace talks."

"Will you inform General Saleh that Atwah might be here?" Rian stifled a yawn. She'd been up for nearly eighteen hours, and her body was reminding her she needed some sleep.

"No, not until we are sure. When we go back to the safehouse tomorrow, we'll get more answers and decide what to do from there." He walked over to her chair and set his hand on her shoulder. "I'll need you with me tomorrow. No one is better at spotting a lie than you are. We may need your skill."

"You think Griffin Force will lie to us?" Rian sat up straighter at that. Maybe her reaction to Augie had been warranted after all.

"No, not lie. But perhaps not tell the whole truth." He looked down at her. He was the man she'd fought beside for the last few years, and who had no idea she wasn't the boy he thought she was. She didn't feel guilty about it. Posing as a boy was for her own survival.

"You seem tense," Malek said, his eyes moving over her face. "Is there something you haven't told me about Khattalah?"

"No, I'm just tired. It's been a difficult day." Rian stood and they walked to the door together. "In order for the peace talks to work, the general will have to transfer the oil port back to the Prime Minister's control. Is he prepared to do that?"

Malek nodded. "I think we're all hopeful that if we give into these demands now, we can have a democratic election that results in a government that will help us all. That's what General Saleh is hoping for, anyway."

"It's what I'm hoping for as well. But I know many good men sacrificed their lives in the fight for those ports. I don't want them forgotten." Rian had almost been forced to fight for the oil port, but Malek had stepped in to keep her near him. She would have surely been killed if she'd gone.

"They won't be." Malek gave her a speculative glance. "Are you okay? I admit, I was surprised at your reaction to Griffin Force's analyst. Augie, I think his name was? You seemed quite agitated." Malek unlocked the door and put his hand on the knob but didn't turn it. "Was there a problem between you two?"

"No. He was asking too many questions, that's all." Rian shrugged her shoulders. "I gave him a reminder that it's good to hold your tongue."

Malek's gaze probed hers, and she met it head on. If she was going to convince him she was fine, she had to act like it. "Okay. We'll put that all behind us. I'll need you focused tomorrow." His voice was quiet, but still commanding.

"I will be. I just need some sleep, that's all." Rian looked up at Malek. He was like the protective older brother she'd always wished for. "I won't let you down."

"You never have." He opened the door, but didn't pull it wide. "The sooner we help Abby and her friends, the sooner they can leave and we can be about the business of winning peace for Libya."

"Peace." She could barely breathe out the word and let herself hope. They'd fought for so long. "Can we really have that again?"

"You must really be tired to ask me that." Malek chuckled. "Usually, you're the one reminding me that we can achieve peace if we work hard enough." He opened the door wide enough that he could fit through and then turned in the doorway. "We'll get there, Rian, don't worry. And you will have a long life ahead of you."

Rian bowed her head. "Here's to both of us having a long life to look forward to."

Malek nodded and disappeared down the dark hallway. Rian shut and locked the door, then went to her bedroom. Not bothering to turn on a light, she took off her keffiyeh, vest, and tunic and undressed down to the shirt she wore underneath. After taking off the bindings on her chest, relief flooded her. Putting her shirt back on, she lay on the bed. In the darkness and shadows, alone, she could be the woman she was. But by day, in anyone's company, she had to appear as a young man. That was the sacrifice she had chosen in order to keep herself safe as well as join the fight to restore order to her country.

She turned over and hugged the pillow. Everything they'd been working for was within their reach if the peace talks could go smoothly. Having an American with a team of commandos show up at the last moment was like finding a stone in the middle of her Usban sausage---tough to chew and harder to swallow. But if they were right and Atwah really was here, the peace talks were in a much more precarious position than anyone knew. Yes, she would help them as Malek had asked. The logical first step was finding out who had come to the training camp three days ago. But her mind couldn't come up with any scenarios on how exactly they would do that. She closed her eyes. Tomorrow would come soon enough and she had to be as prepared as she could. No distractions.

An image of Augie popped into her head, his voice echoing in her mind: *"I think you're hiding something."*

Yes, she was hiding something. But probably not what he was thinking. She turned onto her back, a feeling of restlessness not letting her relax. How would Augie react if he knew what her secret was? Hopefully she would never find out. Rian had to do everything she could to keep her true identity a secret, because if she didn't, her life would be forfeit. And though she would give her life for the cause for freedom, she wasn't ready to die just because it was safer to be a young man engaged in the fight than a Libyan woman dependent on others for even basic necessities.

No, she had done what she had to do and would continue to keep her secret. Which meant she had to help the Griffin Force team to find their information so they could leave.

As soon as possible.

CHAPTER THREE

A ugie lifted his head off the desk and winced at the pain in his neck. He rubbed the spot, wishing he'd walked the five steps over to the cot in the corner and slept there last night. He'd wanted to look at one more site for any chatter of Atwah being in Libya, so when Rian and Malek came back in the morning, they'd have one more bit of evidence that he was here. But before he could bring up the monitoring site, the electricity had clicked off, and instead of setting up the generator, he'd fallen asleep hoping it would come back on.

The electricity was on now, though. Clicking over to several sites, he checked his alerts, and when he didn't see anything new, he stood and stretched. He reached over to pull the heavy curtain away from the window slightly to let a sliver of light in. The dirty window made the sky look even more gray, as if even the sun was struggling to get up and shine this morning. Everything he'd seen of Libya so far had been tinged with gray, as if the very country itself was exhausted from the years of war.

He slowly rolled his shoulders and headed for the door. Voices were coming from the kitchen area, so he followed them down the hall and through the kitchen doorway.

"Sleeping Beauty has awakened," Nate said, as he took a piece of bread and a few dates from the serving plate in front of him. "You looked dead to the world when I checked on you half an hour ago."

"Long night," he said, eyeing the food.

"There's bread, dates, and an MRE on the breakfast menu." Nate moved toward the table and sat down on a rickety wooden chair that looked like it could fall apart at any moment.

Augie replaced Nate at the counter and took one of the breakfast MREs. He'd never minded eating the ready-to-eat meals, and the breakfast one had a few of his favorites in it like oatmeal and fig bars.

"Find any other intel on Atwah last night?" Colt asked, as he joined Nate at the table.

"A few obscure files on his time in Guantanamo." Augie helped himself to a few dates from the plate on the counter to go with his MRE. "Nothing that would help us track him down while he's in Libya."

Abby appeared at his elbow. "I think we'll have to rely on local intelligence for that."

"Speaking of that," Augie started, hesitating for a moment before meeting Abby's eyes. "How much do you trust Malek and his friend? I mean, I know Malek helped us last night, but Rian was acting pretty strangely. And we all know that allegiances around here change all the time."

Abby took an MRE and opened it before she answered. "Colt mentioned that you've got some suspicions about Rian. I don't know him as well as I know Malek, but I trust Malek. We were on a sticky case a few years back, and he really came through for me. He's as solid as they come, in my opinion, and if trusts Rian, then I do, too."

"I tried to run a background check on boys named Rian Dahmani, but couldn't find anything. No birth record, school records, employment, nothing. Don't you think that's odd?" Augie set the date down on his plate. He knew in his bones that something was off about the guy, but he couldn't explain it.

Abby tilted her head as if to consider his words. "The country has been at war for a decade and records can be lost or misplaced. The best we can do is keep an eye on Rian. We need Malek's help. He's well connected to General Saleh and his followers and we won't get far without that network. He's our only asset on the ground that can help us find Atwah." She opened a cupboard to get out a glass.

There were two distinct knocks on the door, and everyone in the room froze for a moment. After a brief pause, three more taps sounded, and the team visibly relaxed.

The lock turned and Malek and Rian walked in. "Good morning." Malek looked at Abby. "I'm glad to see you all again. I hope you slept well."

Rian held up a small bag. "We stopped at the market, and they had fresh mango juice this morning, so we bought some for our meeting."

Malek led the way and Rian followed him over to the table, where they both sat down. Abby brought over two glasses for them and then took a seat next to Nate. Colt kept his position near the sink, as if he were presiding over this meeting. Augie didn't sit, but made sure he had a good vantage point near Colt to watch Rian from.

Colt spoke first. "Well, like I mentioned last night, we believe

Atwah is here at a training camp just outside Benghazi. His organization has had some pretty big setbacks, and our intel says he's going to ground and using Libya to hide in."

Malek looked at Rian, who gave him a small nod. "We also received some intel last night. Someone was smuggled into the training camp three nights ago. We don't know who, but they must be someone important. Two guards bring them food and supplies, and no one else is allowed near the bunker."

"That would line up with when we think Atwah landed in Libya," Augie said, a little relief going through him that his intel had been spot on. But his feeling didn't last long.

"No one has seen who is in the bunker. It may or may not be Atwah." Rian took a sip of mango juice, but kept his eyes on Augie, as if trying to see how the news affected him. Augie made sure his face remained impassive. He wasn't going to wear his feelings so openly.

"Do we know how many people are currently at the training camp?" Nate asked, giving Augie a puzzled look before turning to face Malek.

"The camp is nearly at capacity right now because we're getting ready to transfer the oil port back to the Prime Minister's Government of National Accord prior to the peace talks. We're training the teams that will replace the ones currently there. The General wants to make sure we have our best men on site." Malek turned the glass around in his hands, but didn't take a drink.

"We just need confirmation it's Atwah and then we can mobilize our team. Brenna and Elliot made contact this morning and are waiting in Egypt for their orders to meet us here." Abby leaned forward over the small square table, trying to catch Malek's eye. "Do you have any contacts at the camp that can help us figure out who is in that bunker?"

"No, not really. The military men who run the camp are a whole different division from what I do in public relations." Malek met her gaze. "I'm more like an organizer who helps get people where they need to be and smooth over any roadblocks that show up. The camp is outside my job description, and so it would be suspicious for me to ask about someone there."

"Would General Saleh know if Atwah were there?" Colt folded his arms across his chest. He wasn't letting any of his feelings show on his face, either.

"I don't know. It's possible. But he's very busy right now getting ready for the peace talks. If anyone close to him is aware, it would be one of his advisors." Malek drank the rest of his juice in one gulp.

Abby twisted around in her seat to look at Colt. "We've got to get someone in there. We can't move until we have confirmation."

"Atwah knows all of us." Nate looked at each person in the room.

Malek shifted in his chair. "Yes, I met him briefly years ago during the beginning of the revolution."

"So, the only person he's never met is Augie." Nate's voice was low, as if he didn't want to say out loud what everyone was thinking.

"And me," Rian said quietly.

The words hung heavy in the air. Augie tried to let them sink in, but his mind was running ahead with possible scenarios. His lungs squeezed, making his heart beat faster. He had to say the words out loud, just to make what he was thinking real. "You want me to go in undercover." It was a statement, not a question.

"How would we even get him in?" Colt asked, looking to Malek. "Is there a way to safely insert him and be able to pull him out?"

Malek stroked his chin again and again, watching Augie carefully. "Possibly. But it would be very dangerous for an American."

He hesitated, and Augie wanted to shout at him to just say it. To tell everyone what his plan was. Yet part of him wanted Malek to stay silent, so there wouldn't be any plan at all. There was nothing to do but wait for Malek to speak, the seconds seeming like hours.

"What is it?" Abby finally prompted.

"A team of revolutionaries occasionally kidnaps high-value targets for ransom. The head of the team could be bribed to say he kidnapped Augie in Egypt and dumped him at a prison that feeds into the training camp. Then he would wait until his transfer to the camp. We could say the General must decide what to do with him, since he's American." Malek eyed Rian before he spoke again. "Rian could go with him. His presence wouldn't be questioned, since everyone knows he's with us, and that could be how you communicate with Augie."

Abby leaned forward, her brow furrowed. "How long would he be kept at the prison? And who are these revolutionaries, exactly? Can they be trusted?" She clasped her hands together on the table. Augie had found she did that with her hands when she was nervous or trying to make a big decision. Somehow, seeing that was comforting to him. She was asking the questions that he couldn't think clearly enough to ask himself right now.

"He wouldn't be kept longer than twenty-four hours," Malek said carefully, staring down at his glass. He cleared his throat before he met Abby's eyes. "And the revolutionaries are a mix of several different groups who want Libya's natural resources."

"I'm guessing that there are some ISIS and al-Qaeda members included in those groups?" Colt asked, his voice low.

"Yes." Malek shifted in his chair. "Circumstances in this war are difficult for outsiders to grasp. We have done what we must, dealt with groups and ideologies that we might not have even considered if we hadn't been at war. But most leaders of these groups care only for money. The team of revolutionaries that I think would be willing to take Augie to the camp will do what I ask for the right price and some good vodka."

"It's risky putting an American in terrorists' hands." Colt glanced over at Augie. "You wouldn't have a weapon, comms, or back up. And we can't risk putting a tracker on you. If it was discovered, you'd be killed on the spot."

Augie's heart skipped a beat. He'd always been the one supporting the team and making sure they got home safe. This time, he would be in the field with some very dangerous people. "If I don't go in, what are the options for getting any information on Atwah?"

"We'll wait for word from Malek and Rian. They get new intel every day." Abby looked to Nate. "Brenna was reaching out to her contacts today. We might get something from her as well."

Nate looked over at Augie. "I think it's your choice. You would be taking a pretty big risk. If you can't do it, we'll just figure out another way like we always do."

Fear rushed over him, but at the same time he knew he was going to do it. His team needed him, and he wasn't going to let them down. "So, what do I need to do exactly once I get to the training camp?"

Colt puffed out a breath, looking a little troubled at the thought of this mission, too. "Just keep your eyes and ears open. See if you can ID Atwah or either of the men with him. Observe, report, and get out of there. If we can, we'll have you report to Rian, and the moment you feel any danger at all, we'll pull you out."

That didn't comfort him at all. Augie looked at Rian. Could he trust him with his life? He didn't think so.

Not that he had a choice.

"Okay, I'll do it." He nodded his head for emphasis. "But if this is going to work, we're going to have to make an airtight cover so that anyone who looks at me will see someone who was important enough to kidnap for ransom."

"I can help with that," Abby said. She got up from her chair and laid her hand on Augie's arm. "You can do this, Aug. And we'll be right behind you."

"Thanks for the vote of confidence," Augie said, putting a smile on his face. "You know, I've been waiting for my chance to show you all how this is done. This will be the quickest ID the team has ever seen, then you guys can put Atwah back in prison."

Nate chuckled. "This is your time to shine, then."

Abby took a step back and gave Augie a once-over. "Well, the first thing we have to do is dirty you up a bit, so you'll look like you were kidnapped in Egypt. We'll definitely leave the stubble."

"Dirty and scruffy. Sounds like the Augie I know." Nate quirked an eyebrow and tilted his head at Colt. "Right?"

Colt laughed. "That aspect of the op might be hard for you, Augie. I know how much personal hygiene and looking your best means to you. But it's for a good cause."

Augie looked at his friends who were more like family to him. "I think I can handle it for a few days."

Abby smiled. "I know you can. But making you look like a hostage is the easy part."

"What's the hard part?" Augie asked, the good feeling disappearing.

Colt stepped up to his other side, his hand on Augie's shoulder. "The hard part will be handing you over to ISIS mercenaries so you get arrested and thrown in a Libyan jail."

Augie swallowed hard and caught Rian staring at him. Whether he liked it or not, he was going on a dangerous mission with someone he didn't trust to have his back. But there was no other choice.

The only thing keeping him from changing his mind and saying no was that if he was successful, they had a chance to recapture the most wanted terrorist in the world.

And that was enough for him to stay in the fight.

CHAPTER FOUR

R ian could feel the tension coming off of Augie as he sat
at the table. His fingers were tapping against his thigh
as Abby applied a little more dirt to his pale cheek.
She'd never seen anyone with hair as red as his and skin that light.
He had a few freckles that dotted his nose, but Abby was
studiously covering them all with soil from the front yard.

"Why do hostages have to be dirty?" he asked, letting out a
breath.

"It's a dirty business." Abby grinned at him. "You'll be fine."

Rian touched her own cheek. She often rubbed dirt on her face
because no one looked twice at a dirty boy on the street. It was a
survival tactic she'd learned early on when she'd started dressing
as a boy years before.

Malek walked in the room and gave Augie an approving look.
"We need to leave if we're going to make the meeting with Omar.
He doesn't like to be kept waiting."

Rian held back a shiver. Omar al-Jaburi was a hardened ISIS
leader. He was the kind of man that looked like he'd been born

with a gun in his hand, and he had no regard for anyone's comfort but his own. But Malek was right. He could be bribed where many other men couldn't. They needed him.

Malek walked forward and motioned for Augie to stand up. He took a zip tie out of his pants pocket.

Augie obediently held out his hands and watched as Malek tightened them over his wrists. "How do I look?"

"Like a hostage." Malek said matter-of-factly and turned to Rian. "Are you ready?"

She nodded and stood as well. They started for the door, but Colt stopped in front of Augie.

"Remember, this is an observe-and-report mission. We need you back safely." Colt's voice was gruff, but Rian could see the caring in his eyes. Augie was important to him.

"Worried you won't be able to access your email without me around? Or help you figure out your social media accounts?" Augie's weak attempt at humor lightened the moment as Colt chuckled. "Don't worry. I'm wearing my lucky plaid shirt. I'll be fine." The two men nodded to each other with an unspoken farewell.

Colt handed Malek a stack of hundred-dollar bills. "For the bribe."

Malek took the money without hesitation and shoved it in the messenger bag hanging over his shoulder. Once that was secure, he took Augie's arm and led him outside. Rian followed. She watched Malek put Augie in the back seat of the van before she climbed in the driver's seat. As an aide to Malek, it would be expected for her to be his driver. Once he was settled in the passenger seat, she started the van and drove off.

The sun had started to sink into the horizon, adding some red and orange to the mostly brown tones of the city. The road was dusty as they left the city and not many other cars were on the road. Rian turned onto the highway that would take them to Suluq, a town that Omar al-Jaburi had made his headquarters. Al-Jaburi---the Omar they knew, and the one who sometimes kidnapped people for ransom---liked the thought of being associated with Omar Mukhtar, the Libyan Resistance Leader from the 1930s. Mukhtar had been hanged in Suluq after fighting for Libyan freedom and finally captured. Omar al-Jaburi tried to make it seem as if he were continuing Mukhtar's mission of fighting for freedom, but privately, Rian thought there was nothing in common with the two men. Omar Mukhtar was a national hero, uniting the Libyan people against foreign invasion and working to secure their independence. Omar al-Jaburi thought only of himself and did everything he could to gain money and power. He had a blackness to his soul that could be frightening if he turned on you.

The three of them were mostly silent on the drive, each lost in their own thoughts of what was to come. When they made it to the outskirts of Suluq, Rian found the deserted road Omar had set as their meeting place. A four-door sedan was already there waiting. Rian pulled in and parked. Omar and two of his men emerged from the car and stood next to it, waiting for them.

"No matter what happens, just stay calm," Malek told Augie. "We'll be doing our best to track you at all times."

Augie swallowed and nodded. He didn't look reassured by those words, but he squared his shoulders. "Don't worry. I'm good."

The tremor in his voice belied his words, but Rian could relate, especially after seeing Omar through the dirty windshield. He was tall, muscular, and his hard features were set in a permanent angry frown.

She got out of the car and joined Malek and Augie, who were a few steps in front of her. Omar met them halfway, a sneer on his face.

"This is the American you told me about?" He gave Augie a once-over. "I expected more."

Malek took the messenger bag from his shoulder. "I just need you to deliver him to the prison and say you picked him up in Egypt, as we agreed. You have brought him for ransom, as you have done many times before. The General will take care of the rest."

Rian looked between the two men, who were nearly toe-to-toe with each other. She'd always admired how calm Malek was, no matter who he was speaking with, whether it was the General or a mercenary like Omar. Perhaps the constant danger they'd been in fighting this war had erased his fear. It hadn't done that for her. Her heart was galloping so hard right then she had to suck in a deep breath to try and slow it down.

Omar took the bag from Malek and opened it. He pulled out the money stack, and his face briefly lost its glower as his lips curved up into an almost smile. He put the money back in and reached for the vodka. His half-smile turned into a grin. "I don't know how you do it. This vodka should be impossible to get!" He turned to his two men and held it up. "Tonight, we'll celebrate!"

They laughed along with Omar, but the sound sent a chill up Rian's spine. Hopefully they would hold off celebrating until Augie had been dropped off at the prison.

Malek moved next to her. "I don't like the look of this. Augie might need our help sooner than we think," he whispered near her ear. "I think you should go with Augie into the prison. Something doesn't feel right."

Rian's ribcage squeezed. She knew Malek was right, but fear rushed over her. Keeping her secret would be even harder in a prison with no privacy and dozens of men incarcerated there. But she couldn't tell Malek that. "Of course, I'll stay with him."

Malek put his hand on her shoulder. "Be safe, my friend."

She nodded, swallowing her fears and objections that she couldn't voice. She'd spent her life following orders, knowing it could cost her everything. This was just another mission.

Omar turned back to Malek. "I don't know what you have planned, but your deviousness surprises and delights me." He stepped forward and grabbed Augie's arm. He started in surprise at being pulled forward.

"Remember, the General does not want him injured." Malek's voice was firm, but Omar only laughed.

"He'll make it to the prison as promised." One of Omar's men handed him a hood, which Omar put over Augie's head.

"Just to make sure, I'm sending my representative along. He's to remain with the American at all times to make sure you keep up our end of the agreement." Malek motioned to Rian who stepped forward. "Then he'll report back to me and the General."

Omar acknowledged what Malek said with a dip of his head, but he didn't reply. Pulling Augie toward the car, he shoved him in the back and then stepped away so Rian could squeeze in beside Augie. She was nearly smashed into Augie's side as one of Omar's men got in from the other side of Augie and took up most of the space. She pressed as far as she could against the door. Omar's second guard sat in the passenger seat, and Omar drove. With all five seats taken, the car seemed cramped and airless. Rian began to feel a bit of anxiety at being in such close quarters, and her breathing quickened. She fought to keep her breaths even, but as the car started and Malek's form got smaller and smaller as they drove away, it became harder. Part of her wished she'd stayed behind with Malek and made up some excuse as to why she couldn't go.

Augie must have sensed her distress. He leaned over and whispered through his hood, "You okay?"

Unwilling to admit that anything was wrong when she was

supposed to be the one reassuring him, she moved even farther toward the door to put a few more millimeters of distance between them. "I'm fine," she ground out from between her teeth.

But when she looked into the front seat, her stomach plummeted. Omar had pulled out the vodka and had popped the top off. Taking a swig, the car veered to the left, and he laughed.

It was still half an hour's drive to the prison. If he drank all the way there, he'd be drunk and more volatile than normal. The chances of them making it safely were decreasing with every swallow. But there was nothing she could do, so she tried to brace herself as best she could for any drunken swerves of the car.

Omar drank his fill, then passed the bottle around to his two men. Once he shared the alcohol, his demeanor seemed more celebratory than angry, and that calmed Rian's fears somewhat. Her arm that was squashed against the door was falling asleep, and Rian couldn't wait to be out of the vehicle.

After what felt like an eternity, they finally made it to the makeshift prison. Omar parked haphazardly in front of the prison door and stumbled out of the driver's seat, before righting himself and straightening his uniform jacket. He seemed tipsy, but not full drunk, so that was probably why they'd made it to the prison in one piece.

His man dragged Augie out from the opposite side of the car, so Rian opened her door and circled the car to follow them. They were laughing and weaving as the outer guard announced their arrival to the prison warden.

The former factory-turned-prison smelled of human sweat and sawdust. What goods had once been made here for her countrymen? Before the years of war had turned it into a building of despair for men who were most likely being held on some infraction that wouldn't merit a prison sentence during peacetime? But she'd learned long ago that some battles couldn't be fought right then and would have to wait their turn. If the peace talks were successful, the healing of her nation could begin, and factories would once again be filled with workers instead of prisoners. She had to believe that.

The warden was waiting for them inside his office and stood when they arrived. "What have we here, Omar?" His large belly jiggled when he spoke, and the reverence in his voice told Rian he knew not to cross Omar.

"I have an American for you that is of interest to the General. Picked him up in Egypt. An American computer hacker." He pushed Augie forward, and he barely caught himself from running into the warden's desk.

The warden's eyes lit up. "A hacker?" He stared at Augie. "He'd fetch a high price on the open market if we could prove he had the skills."

Omar tilted his head as if considering the warden's words. He nodded toward the warden's computer. "We could do a little test?"

Rian shifted uneasily. This wasn't part of the plan. "I'm sure the General would prefer he be escorted to a cell immediately."

Neither man listened to her. Omar grabbed Augie's shoulder and shoved him into the warden's chair. He took off the hood and leaned close to Augie. "If you are the hacker you claim to be, you would be able to show us, no?"

Augie looked around the room, stopping briefly on her face before meeting Omar's gaze. "I suppose."

The warden walked over to Augie's other side. "Hack into my commander's email." He wrote something on a piece of paper, then pushed it over to Augie.

Relief briefly flashed over Augie's features before he held up his hands. Omar took out a knife and cut the zip tie off. "Hurry up," he growled.

Augie flexed his fingers. He began tapping at the keyboard and within moments, he sat back with a smile. "There you go."

The warden leaned in and began to scroll through his commander's emails. Stopping at one, he clicked on it and read the message, his face getting redder by the minute.

Omar looked over his shoulder and shook his head at the words on the screen. "He isn't giving you the promotion."

"That promotion was mine," the warden hissed. "How could he give it to Khaled? The man can barely tie his own shoes." He began to pace the room.

"Just change the email to give it to yourself," Omar said with a wave of his hand.

Augie shook his head. "We can't do that. Then he'll know he was hacked."

The warden slammed his fist down on the desk. "I don't care if he knows. Change the name on that promotion so it says I got it."

"The email has already been sent. It wouldn't do any good to send another one with your name on it. That would only be suspicious." Augie leaned back a bit and held his hands up as Omar approached. "You wouldn't want your boss knowing you'd peeked at his personal correspondence, would you?"

Omar lifted him out of the chair by his shirt and pushed him against the wall. "You'll do what we say."

"Listen---" Augie started, but Omar drew back his fist. Augie moved slightly to the left just as Omar's punch grazed Augie's jaw. He slumped against the wall, holding his face. Omar moved forward, but Rian got between them, her hands out.

"The General specifically asked that no harm come to this man." She met Omar's black eyes. They seemed like an endless abyss of darkness and chilled her to the core. She moved her gaze to his forehead. "You will answer to the General for any injuries to this man."

Omar stepped back, but kept his eyes on Augie. "Punching an American was on my, how do you say it? My bucket list." His hands clenched into tight fists once more and Rian moved forward to stand in front of Augie. She couldn't allow him to be hit again.

Augie placed his hand on her shoulder and pushed himself in front of her. "Well, I'm glad I helped you cross that off your list. Hey, you know, I don't know you guys very well, but things got serious pretty fast in here. Let's see if I can lighten things up a little. Since we're trading personal bucket lists and all."

Omar folded his arms and no one else spoke, so Augie continued. "I've always dreamed of being a comedian, so here goes." He paused and took a deep breath, looking at each face in the room. "It's great to be with you here tonight. As you all know, I'm a computer hacker. And a guest in your prison. But let's say I escaped and someone asked you where I went, you could say, I have no idea, he just *ransomware*."

The room was silent, but Augie let out a nervous chuckle. "Get it? Ran . . . some . . . where?"

Rian gave a low laugh and Augie looked back at her and smiled. "Well, my hacker friends loved that one. But hey, thanks for having me tonight. I'll be here until tomorrow."

"Yes, you will. No one will be escaping, hacker or no." Omar turned to the warden. "I'll escort them both down to the cells since the boy was tasked to remain with the prisoner until he's transferred to the camp tomorrow."

The warden made a noise of agreement before sitting heavily in his chair to stare gloomily at his computer. Omar and his men frog-marched Augie and Rian down a steep set of stairs. They ended up in a long room that had been sectioned off into small cells with concrete walls between each one and an open door that was covered by iron bars from floor to ceiling. The cells looked like large animal cages. Rian held in a shiver.

Their group stopped at the far end. One of Omar's men held out a ring of keys and Omar took them to unlock the last two cell doors.

"You'll be in separate cells. I find there's less insubordination when people are by themselves. And we wouldn't want anyone leaving before it's time, or doing any ransomware tricks now would we? You wouldn't want to miss your ride to the camp tomorrow." He leaned close to Rian and it was all she could do not to shrink away. "Then you can give a report to your boss that I held my end of the agreement."

"See that you do, or my report will not reflect well on you." She adjusted her keffiyeh and walked into the cell. Augie was practically thrown in, but she couldn't see anything else once she was in her cell. At least she was situated right next to Augie.

She listened for their footsteps to recede down the hall, then she went to the corner of her cell where she could barely see the opposite corner of Augie's. "Augie?" she said quietly. "How is your jaw?"

He came to the corner as well. They couldn't see each other with the concrete wall between them, but they were right next to each other and could talk quietly. "I've taken a punch before. I'm fine."

She sank down to the floor, relieved that they'd both made it through that ordeal. "Good. I'm glad."

Augie was silent. Was he upset? Did he blame her? She was just about to move away when he spoke. "I know we're not friends, but thanks for standing up for me back there."

His words warmed her. "I know I look small, but Malek taught me to fight. I think we could have held our own."

Augie's chuckle echoed through the room. "I don't know. Did you see Omar's first lieutenant? He looked like he had so many layers of muscles on his arms that any punches we threw would bounce off like quarters. And he had no neck at all. That can't be normal."

Rian laughed. His description was pretty accurate. They were quiet again, but this time the silence wasn't uncomfortable. "You asked me last night if I was recruited to the cause or coerced." Did he remember? Would bringing up their conversation make him suspicious of her again? She hoped not. "The answer is neither. I was born in Benghazi, and I've never left Libya. Fighting for our freedom and independence is all I've ever known and wanted for a very long time."

Augie's voice seemed closer when he spoke next. "I'm from the great state of Virginia, but I've lived all over. I've always wanted to change the world for the better somehow, and help people like you find the freedom I've always had. I know that might sound corny or idealistic, but it's true. It's just always been a part of who I am."

His words pierced her soul. What would freedom feel like? If the peace talks worked, they'd still be a long way away from a free country, but it was a needed first step. And maybe people like Augie and Griffin Force could help the process along. Perhaps she had misjudged him. "Do you have any more jokes?"

He laughed softly. "I think my dream of being a comedian died in the warden's office. I didn't even get a courtesy laugh!"

"I laughed very hard on the inside," she assured him. "But if you cannot think of any more jokes, I have one for you." She fiddled with the edge of her keffiyeh, trying to remember all the details of the joke Malek had told her not long ago. "There was a huge hole in the ground in downtown Tarhuna and people kept falling in and getting hurt. Citizens were complaining quite loudly about it, so the city council decided to gather the three wisest men in the city to find solutions to the problem.

"The first wise man's solution was to park some ambulances right next to the hole, so that when anyone fell in, they could be rushed to the hospital right away. The second wise man had a better idea, that instead of having an ambulance wait by the hole, and wasting time transporting injured patients, they would build a hospital right next to the hole and treat any injured people right away. The third wise man was thinking for a while, then he confidently said that instead of wasting the city's resources on ambulances or making a new hospital, they'd just cover the hole up and dig one right next to the existing hospital." A giggle bubbled up inside her at the absurdness of the story just as it had when Malek had related it to her.

Augie laughed, the warmth of his tone washing over her. She liked his laugh. "You know, this is such a small world. We have almost the exact same joke in Virginia, only for us it's Richmond and for you, it's Tarhuna." He chuckled. "Sometimes I miss being home."

"What do you miss about it?" She leaned her back against the wall. He really did have a nice voice.

"I miss my mom's Brunswick stew. It's like a little bit of heaven on earth. And I miss the Blue Ridge Mountains. It's the most beautiful place I've ever seen." His voice was wistful. "The majesty of those mountains still inspires me. I could spend weeks hiking them, fishing the streams, and just enjoying the beauty of it all."

Rian closed her eyes. She couldn't really imagine the mountains and streams he spoke of, but she did remember sitting down to a favorite meal with her mother. It had been so long since she'd allowed herself to think of such things. "Benghazi was beautiful once. I remember going to the beach and looking at the sea and thinking I'd never seen anything so blue. And my mother took me to the Roman ruins nearby when I was little, and she told me stories of those who had lived here before us." A bolt of longing went through her. That had been such a simpler time. Before she knew the heartache of loss.

"Where is your mother now?" Augie's voice was hardly more than a whisper.

"She died in the war." Rian didn't want to think of her, of the life they'd dreamed of living one day that would never happen now.

"My father died, too," Augie said softly. "Fighting in Iraq."

A little piece of her heart cracked open at his confession. He'd experienced some of the pain she had, and Rian hadn't been expecting that. What would an American man know of loss and war? But he did.

"I'm sorry." She wanted to reach her hand through the bars and around the edge of the wall to give him some comfort. But she didn't think that was something a young man would do, so she folded her hands in her lap.

He was quiet for another moment, and Rian could hear some rustling as if he was moving closer to the floor. "Guess we might as well get some sleep while we can."

"Yes." She lay down as well and pulled her sleeves down over her hands. They needed to be ready for what tomorrow would bring, but she couldn't stop thinking about the man in the cell next to her. He was so very unexpected. He'd said they weren't friends, but what if they could be? With a shake of her head, she crossed her arms around herself. She was masquerading as a young man. No one could get close to her or her secret would be revealed and the punishment would be death.

But in that moment, she let herself dream. Tomorrow and all its reality would come soon enough. Just for tonight, in a dark cell in Libya, she had a friend.

CHAPTER FIVE

A few little shafts of light from the high, narrow windows pierced the darkness of the basement cells they were in. Augie groaned and rolled to his back. He'd thought falling asleep at a table had been hard on his neck and back, but sleeping on a concrete floor was much worse. He'd tossed and turned most of the night, trying to find a comfortable position, but there wasn't one. Slowly sitting up, he stretched his aching back, then gingerly touched his throbbing jaw. Omar had packed quite a punch. Luckily, Augie had dodged the full force of the blow and been able to keep all of his teeth. Testing his pain threshold, he opened and closed his mouth. It was bearable, but he might not be able to chew anything for a while. Not that anyone was offering him food.

Augie tilted his head toward the bars of the cell. He didn't hear anything from the cell next door. Was Rian awake? "Rian?"

He kept his voice low, just in case the kid was actually getting some sleep. Having him around had actually been comforting for Augie. Their conversation last night had made him think they could actually be friends. Seeing Rian stand between him and Omar had made him rethink any suspicions Augie had been harboring. He'd stood up for Augie and put himself in the line of fire. Augie wasn't going to forget that.

The metal doors at the end of the hall clanged open. "Rian," Augie called, louder this time.

He stood up, ready for whomever was coming down that hall. "Rian." He made one last attempt to get the guy up and ready as well.

"I'm here." Rian's voice was groggy, as if he'd just awakened. Had he been able to get a decent night's sleep on the concrete then?

"Someone's coming," Augie warned.

They both waited for the footsteps to get closer. It didn't take long for a guard to appear in front of the cells, a key ring in his hands. He was dressed in an odd mishmash of different military uniforms. He had the distinctive blue camouflage jacket from the Iranian army with an Egyptian army beret. His pants were the brown camouflage of the Libyan army. Augie frowned. Why would he have so many different uniforms? Were there not enough Libyan ones to go around? Had he served in those countries? Killed soldiers from those countries? Augie wanted to ask, but when he saw the gun at the guard's side, he kept quiet.

The guard unlocked Augie's cell first and then Rian's. "Come forward," he ordered.

They did, and he motioned for them to hold out their hands. He zip tied their wrists together, ran a wand over both of them to check for trackers, then pointed toward the door. "We are going upstairs to the van. You are to be quiet and do exactly what you are told."

Rian glanced at Augie and awkwardly rearranged his keffiyeh over his head and around his neck with his zip tied hands. Augie started toward the exit, and Rian stayed close to his side. The guard brought up the rear. They went up the first flight of steps, where another guard joined them with three other men. They all shuffled outside to the waiting van.

Their guard reached for the door handle, then stopped. Turning to look at them, he straightened. "We have just received word that our men are needed at the oil port to ready everything for the peace talks. You will be honored to go to the training camp to fill the positions of those who are leaving. You have the opportunity to fight for your country. For freedom!" His eyes were bright, and Augie couldn't look away. The man definitely believed in his cause. The three other men from the prison gave a weak cheer. They didn't seem as excited as the guard, but were making an effort, at least.

The guard looked at each of them and nodded, then opened the van door. They all silently got in and sat down. Augie's stomach was growling, and he shifted in his seat. At least he had a window seat, unlike the poor guy in the back who was squished between two other prisoners who smelled as if they hadn't bathed in a month or more. Rian was in the other window seat next to him. Were they being given preferential treatment? He couldn't tell.

They drove for about forty-five minutes with nothing more to look at beyond small villages and the occasional clusters of trees to break up the monotonous brown of everything else. Augie's body was aching and his eyes were having a hard time staying open. He was so tired. He leaned against the window and closed his eyes. Just a little rest couldn't hurt anything.

In what seemed like just a few minutes later, Rian poked his leg. "Wake up."

The van had stopped. They were at a checkpoint and a guard was speaking to the driver. Beyond the checkpoint there was a large field with dozens of men marching through drills and formations. This must be the training camp.

The driver must have pressed on the gas pedal as the van lurched through the checkpoint and took them to a small group of rusty brown metal buildings, before he parked. He exited the vehicle and opened their door. All the prisoners filed out. Rian and Augie were immediately separated from the other three.

"This way," the guard of many uniforms said to Rian and Augie, turning on his heel and walking toward a small building. He led them past the metal-looking buildings toward a small concrete bunker near a hill at the edge of the camp. There were several other bunkers spaced evenly apart, the brownish gray of the concrete blending into the hill behind them.

He went to the door of the middle one and opened it. "You will wait here for instructions from the General. If you need to go anywhere on base, you must be escorted by me." He waited until they were inside, then cut their zip ties off. With a brief nod, he shut the door with a bang.

Augie walked the perimeter of the small room, rubbing his wrists. Two cots were opposite each other. A small bathroom in the corner with a sink and a toilet. A metal chair and a flimsy-looking metal folding table.

"They really like metal here, don't they?" He sat down on the chair and watched Rian cross the room. "I only saw four bunkers like this. It shouldn't be too hard to find Atwah if he's in one of them."

"What's the plan for visiting the other three bunkers if we have to be escorted everywhere?" Rian sat cross-legged on one of the cots.

"The door isn't locked. Maybe we could take a look around. If we get caught, we could just say we were looking for our escort." Augie looked at the thin mattress on the cot Rian was sitting on.

After the concrete floor last night, the mattress seemed luxurious.

Rian gave him a curious look. "Do you want to go right now?"

Augie looked away from the cot, staring at the door instead. He wanted to lie down, but he stood up from the chair instead. The sooner they identified Atwah, the sooner he could get out of here. "Why not?"

He cracked the door open and peeked out. No one seemed to be around. The sun was high in the sky, and the air shimmered with the heat. Opening the door a little wider, Augie slipped out and Rian followed. He walked to the side of the bunker and around the corner. The area seemed deserted.

"Are there more bunkers on the other side of the camp? Or are these the only ones?" Augie was beginning to think maybe they were in the wrong place. If Atwah were here, they would see his guards. Had he left?

"No, the other side of the camp is just that training field that we saw on arrival and a large building for sleeping and meals." Rian stayed at his elbow, fiddling with his keffiyeh and maneuvering the large scarf so it covered the bottom of his face. With the dust kicking up around them with every footstep, Augie wished he'd thought of bringing one for himself.

They kept going, searching the perimeter of each bunker until they ended up on the corner of the third bunker trying to get a view of the last one. With a quick peek at the structure, Augie drew back when he spotted two guards sitting at strategic angles on the two most visible corners of the bunker. They were keeping a close watch on anyone who might come near them.

"I think we found him," Augie said softly, his heart rate kicking up. This was it.

"Now what?" Rian looked up at him.

Augie looked around them. There wasn't anywhere nearby that

they could go that wouldn't alert the guards to their presence. Looking skyward, Augie noticed the bunker's flat roof. "What about climbing up there? Then we could get a better vantage point to try and listen to their conversation."

Rian's gaze followed his and he swallowed. "Give me a push."

Augie grinned. The kid had guts. He put his hands together, and Rian stuck his foot in. Boosting him up, Rian neatly caught the edge of the roof and pulled himself over. He reached down for Augie, but they both heard the footsteps at the same time. Rian drew back and Augie flattened himself against the corner of the bunker. It wasn't much cover, but that was all he could do.

The officer that had escorted them to the camp walked by with a man dressed as a Libyan military commander at his side. Neither of them gave the third bunker, where Rian and Augie were hiding, a glance.

Breathing a sigh of relief, Augie waited a moment, then poked his head around the corner. The guards surrounding the bunker were opening the door for the commander and the officer. They blocked the doorway for a moment while they spoke, and then the guards fell back and Augie saw the man they'd been hunting for months standing there in the doorframe.

Atwah.

Before Augie could blink, however, Atwah melted back into the bunker, and the door was shut.

Had he really seen him? Augie rubbed his eyes. He was tired, but not that tired. That had definitely been Atwah. He'd had the signature black beard with silver streaks running along the edges and the jet-black turban he always wore on his head. It was him.

Hearing rustling from the roof, Augie looked up. Rian had shimmied back to the edge of the roof and heaved himself over, landing on his feet next to Augie

"Did you see him?" Rian asked, dusting off his hands.

"You saw him, too?" Good. Augie hadn't been imagining things.

"From what I could hear, the guards were talking about travel arrangements, so Atwah won't be here long. With the camp moving out tomorrow, it's likely he'll go with them." Rian's eyes flashed with anger. "His presence here can only mean one thing: he's here to sabotage the peace talks, I'm sure of it. We need to get word to Malek and your team."

"Let's get back to our bunker before we're caught and ruin everything." Augie began to walk as quickly as he could without drawing any attention to them. The mission was over. They'd done it. Atwah was here. Now they just had to figure a way to get back to Benghazi.

Rian was nearly running to keep up with him, but they made it back to the bunker without seeing anyone. Once inside, Augie sat down in the chair and rubbed his hand over his face. "We did it."

Rian had resumed his position on the cot. "Malek said there's a supply van that will be leaving the camp tomorrow morning. We need to make sure we're on it. With the camp moving out, we shouldn't be missed."

Augie couldn't help the feeling of triumph running through him. "And once we're back, I'm going to stick to being behind my computer during ops." Even the thought of resuming his normal support position for the team sent a rush of relief over him.

"You didn't like being out of the field? I thought we were a pretty good team." Rian gave him a small smile, and it felt like he was offering a sort of olive branch. A follow-up from last night, in a way.

Augie returned the smile, hoping Rian could see he was sincere. "We made a great team. Thanks for having my back." Remembering his earlier mistrust, he took a breath and met Rian's gaze. "I'm sorry for how I acted when we first met."

Rian shook his head. "I wasn't myself either. I'm glad we can have a fresh start." He looked around the room. "So, now we just have to wait until tomorrow, and then we can both go our separate ways, but part as friends."

Augie nodded, but the thought of going their separate ways made him sad. He'd bonded with Rian over the last twenty-four hours. "Maybe you and Malek will stick with the team for a while yet. I wouldn't write me off so soon."

Rian yawned. "I didn't sleep very well last night, so I think I might take advantage of the bed, if you don't mind. Wake me if you need to." He met Augie's eyes as if wanting permission.

"I think I'll do the same," Augie said. He stood and walked toward the small sink in the bathroom. "After I splash a bit of water on myself and clean off some of this dust and dirt."

He thought he heard Rian chuckle, but he didn't turn around to check. He twisted the faucet and a small trickle of water dribbled out. Augie didn't care. He cupped his hand and collected enough to run over his face and neck. Barely able to hold back a sigh of pleasure, he worked some of the dirt off his face. With no mirror, he had no idea if he'd gotten all the dirt off, but he felt better.

Walking out, he went over to the other cot and lay down. He folded his arms and his eyes closed as if by their own volition. When he awoke, the setting sun was pushing the last of its rays through the one long, narrow window that nearly spanned the width of one wall in the bunker. Augie sat up and stretched. He hadn't meant to sleep so long, but it had helped all the aches in his body.

He stood and walked over to Rian's bunk. His keffiyeh had slipped down to his shoulders, leaving his head and neck uncovered, which never happened when Rian was awake. The guy was always making sure his keffiyeh was in place. His small hands were folded under his cheek as he slept. With the sun's last rays shining on his face, giving his skin an inner glow, Augie looked closer. His brow furrowed as he leaned in. No. It couldn't be. Shock radiated over his body. How had he not seen it before? The smooth skin. The lack of an Adam's apple. The hands. Even the tunic that had twisted over Rian's lower body in sleep revealed a curve of a hip.

Rian was a woman.

He backed up until he was across the room and could sit on his cot. He stared at Rian. He'd felt like something was off from the moment he'd met her. He'd known she was hiding something--- and she had been.

But how long had she been living as a young man? And why?

He needed answers, but before he could ask any questions, the door opened, and the commander who had been with their guard earlier strode in. Augie's eyes flew to Rian. She was awake and alert, redoing her keffiyeh to cover her head and neck and straightening her tunic. The commander looked at both of them as if they were as valuable as the dust on his shoe.

"Get up." His voice was little more than a growl.

Rian and Augie both quickly stood next to their cot.

"You will come with me." The commander turned to leave, but Rian spoke up.

"Sir, I must remind you that we are under the General's protection. He will decide what to do with the American prisoner." She took a step forward. "We have been instructed to wait for word from him."

The commander turned on his heel and quickly advanced on Rian until he was standing over her. Augie moved closer, feeling a protectiveness wash over him. Rian was in terrible danger. His mind raced through possible scenarios. If anyone found out she was a woman, she would be killed. Yet she'd voluntarily come on this mission with him, knowing the risks. He couldn't let her be hurt.

"We are taking you both to the oil port. If the General wishes to meet with you, he will find you there." The commander stared hard at Rian, then put his hands behind his back and turned to speak to Augie. "But until then, you are under my command and I have plans for you."

Augie didn't know what to say and stood there mute. The commander didn't seem to expect an answer, however. He took Rian by the arm and towed her toward the door. Augie didn't need an invitation to follow. He was right behind them, but he stopped when they walked outside.

Atwah stood outside the bunker, waiting for them. His dark eyes met Augie's, drawing him into their coldness, as mesmerizing as a cobra's stare.

"Thank you, commander," Atwah said, his voice as smooth as silk, as if he were wishing those present a good evening. "You've been a great help."

Atwah's two guards came forward. The commander handed Rian over to one, and the other took Augie's arm in a vise-like grip. Everything moved in slow motion as Augie walked forward with the guard, nearly stumbling, watching the smile spread across Atwah's face as each guard forced Rian and Augie to kneel in front of Atwah.

"Kneel until you are told you may rise," one of the guards barked.

Augie tried to catch Rian's eye, but she stared straight ahead as if he wasn't next to her. He clenched his fists in frustration and tried to calm his racing heart. He had to think! There had to be something he could do. He had to protect her. Figure out a way to get a message to Malek or Colt.

But when Augie looked up at a man who had terrorized the world for over a decade, he knew they were both in trouble. Deep, deep trouble. They needed a miracle. Right now.

CHAPTER SIX

Atwah's guard escorted Rian and Augie to a group of soldiers that were in line to board a waiting bus. Augie was acting strangely, and Rian wished they were alone so she could find out what was wrong. Had he seen something? Heard something? What was going on?

When it was nearly their turn to board, Rian saw Omar standing a little way off, watching them. Was he regretting giving them up to Atwah? Had he taken money for the information he'd obviously provided about them? She wouldn't doubt it. Maybe Atwah had the vodka he liked and he'd sold them for a drink. Rian stopped to stare at Omar, unable to hide her anger and disappointment. Not that he would care, but it made her feel better.

At her hesitation, the guard shoved her forward, and she fell to the ground, landing hard on one knee. "Get on the bus," he commanded. He didn't wait for her to stand back up, but grabbed her arm and pulled her to his side. Pain shot up her leg and back, and she could hardly contain a little yelp.

"Hey," Augie said, elbowing his way between the guard and Rian. "There's no call for that." He looked into her face, the concern evident in his eyes. "You okay?"

And that's when she knew. Augie had figured out her secret. There was no other reason for him to start treating her like she was fragile and needed protecting, unless he knew she was a woman. She pursed her lips and opened her eyes wide in a look that she hoped conveyed her message not to reach out like that. He couldn't treat her any differently than he had before, or she would be killed.

"I'm fine." She lifted her chin and pivoted to gingerly put weight on her sore knee and step up onto the bus.

The guard turned his back on Augie and was right behind her. He pointed to a seat in the middle, and once she sat down, he settled next to her. Augie was directed to the seat directly in front of them. He turned around to look at her, but she didn't meet his eyes. How had he guessed? And when? Whatever the answers to those questions were, they couldn't talk about it right now. She had to stay calm and think this through.

When all the seats were filled except the one next to Augie, the bus driver climbed in and started the bus, but let it idle. The doors opened for two final passengers. Atwah and Omar walked down the aisle, greeting several soldiers as they went. Omar sat next to Augie, and Atwah continued to the back where there was a seat on the very last row. What was his endgame? Why was he joining the soldiers on the bus? Obviously, he wanted to disrupt the peace talks, but how? From what she knew about him, he struck fast and hard, and didn't mind killing anyone who stood in his way. Nothing about him being here boded well for anyone.

The guard crowded into her space on the seat, just as Omar's guards had done in the car when Rian and Augie had been delivered to the prison. Was there a bodyguard school that taught them to do that? Rian pressed as close to the window as she could, not wanting to have any part of her touching the guard if she could help it. If they were traveling to the nearest oil terminal, Ras Lanuf, it was going to be at least a four-hour trip. The sun had set, and darkness was settling over them as the bus left the training camp. Rian closed her eyes. She was hungry, but not tired. The nap she'd taken had helped her energy level, since she hadn't slept much at the prison the night before, but there was nothing to do on the bus but think.

She opened her eyes to look at the back of Augie's head. He was leaning against the window as well. They had been so close to finishing the mission and getting back to the safehouse. But now they were on their own and in the company of the most dangerous man in the world.

And Augie knew she was a woman.

She was fairly sure he wouldn't give her secret away intentionally, but the truth was, she didn't know him very well. How much could she trust him? The questions swirled through her mind. She hadn't spent so many years disguising herself only to be revealed now. She had to talk to him the first moment she got and swear him to secrecy. Then, once he left Libya, she would be safe as a boy again.

The bus trundled along the coastal road, but darkness prevented Rian from seeing anything beyond the bits of scrub and trees on the shoulder. The guard next to her was snoring, mingling with several other snores of sleeping men. Rian tried to find a semi-comfortable position, her knee still throbbing a bit from when she'd fallen earlier. Rotating to her side, away from the guard, she froze when she heard whispering behind her. The person was speaking in Arabic, and she strained to hear what they were saying. "Oil terminal" and "General Saleh" were all she could make out.

Peeking over her seat, she saw Atwah leaning forward to talk with four men. Their heads were bent close together. Clearly, they didn't want anyone overhearing them. Atwah lifted his head to look around. Rian quickly slouched down. If only her guard weren't snoring so loudly, she could possibly hear more of what they were saying. She glanced over at him. If she nudged him, would he change position and stop snoring? It was worth a try.

She poked him in the side, but she might as well have been poking a stone. How had Augie described it? She could bounce quarters off muscles like that. She stifled a laugh thinking of that conversation and poked the guard again, harder this time. He grunted and changed position, turning away from her. His snoring stopped and turned to deep breaths.

Rian leaned as close as she could to the back of the seat. The whispering had gotten more intense. This time she heard one of them say, "the men are ready and have been told the terms and the rewards." Another whispered, "undisputed leader," "computer," and "timing the attack." Were they talking about Augie? What attack, and what were the terms and rewards Atwah was offering?

The whispered conversation stopped when the ancient bus ground to a halt. Several soldiers sat up straight and stretched, the vinyl of the seats creaking with their movements. Rian peered out the window, trying to see anything in the darkness. They seemed to be on the edge of a residential area, but with only a few lights, that weren't very illuminating, it was hard to tell. Were they not going directly to the port, then? She frowned, then took a deep breath. No use getting frustrated. She needed to stay alert and ready for any opportunity to escape.

Omar got up and forced Augie to walk in front of him. Rian's guard did the same. They moved down the steps, and a humid breeze stole over her face as she stepped off. She breathed it in as deeply as she could. Being able to stretch her legs and smell something other than stale air from being confined with a full busload of men was something she'd never take for granted again.

A soldier waited near the exit, handing out small strips of jerky, while another soldier handed out *gharayba* nearby. Rian grabbed a few strips of jerky and the two offered cookies before she walked on. She quickly bit into the jerky. It was old and as tasty as a tire tread, but she was so hungry, she didn't care. Chewing slowly, she tried to make the meat strips last as long as she could. The *gharayba* weren't her favorite, either, but the butter cookies had a pistachio on the top of each one, which felt like a special treat.

Augie slowed his step until she'd caught up to him. He'd eaten the cookies first and was still trying to chew a jerky strip. "What kind of meat is this?" he asked, holding up his second strip.

"Lamb." She raised her eyebrows. Had he eaten and enjoyed lamb before or would he wrinkle his nose at it?

"Not bad." He took another bite. "You eat yours already?"

"Yes." She glanced around her. The small, squat concrete row houses were often used for oil terminal workers, but tonight the soldiers were all being herded into them. The houses were lined up in straight lines on either side of the street, and soldiers were being directed into each one, though Omar and her guard marched past most of them without pause.

"Where do you think we're going?" she asked Augie, her voice soft so as to not call her guard's attention to their conversation.

The guard heard her anyway and grabbed her elbow. "Shut up. No more talking."

Rian fell silent, but stayed as close as she could to Augie. It was best for both of them if they stayed together.

When all the other men had been billeted to one of the houses, Rian and Augie were ushered into the very last building. It was a little larger than the others, with a living room, kitchen, several bedrooms, and a closed door down a long hallway. They were marched to the closed door, where it opened into a small, square room that was bare of furniture except for a long metal table and three metal chairs. She'd never really noticed all the metal before Augie had mentioned it, but now she couldn't stop noticing how much there really was.

"Sit," Rian's guard said gruffly. She took the chair closest to her and Augie sat in the one next to it. Omar and the guard stood against the wall, arms folded. Both of them were armed. There would be no escape from here.

They waited in silence. Rian rolled her neck. Waiting was a fact of life in Libya. Waiting for food. Waiting for orders. She'd learned to hold herself in and not give away any feelings of anxiety or impatience, though that control was hanging by a thread at the moment. She had so many things she needed to say to Augie. What exactly did he know about her secret and what did he plan to do with that knowledge?

The door finally opened and Atwah strode in with his other guard. He carried a laptop that he set down on the table before he sat in the empty chair.

"Omar tells me you can hack into email." Atwah's eyes rested on Augie, his black gaze pinning him.

Augie's fingers were tapping on his thigh, which might have been an indication of his nervousness, but outwardly he didn't look cowed by Atwah. Instead, he met his eyes head on. "I'm not sure what you mean."

Omar came forward with a sneer. "Don't play dumb. You know exactly what he means. You had no problem showing us the prison commandant's email."

Atwah held up a hand to silence Omar. "I have paid a great price and brought you here because I need you to hack into

General Saleh's email." His words were soft, but he might as well have shouted, as the order reverberated through the room.

Rian's heart sped up. He couldn't be allowed to see the general's private emails. That could be disastrous for not only the peace talks, but to the fight for a free and united Libya.

Augie shifted in his seat and glanced at the laptop. "Well, the prison thing was an easy hack because of the information the warden already had and the lack of security on his boss's email account. I'm sure General Saleh has layers of security measures." He held out his hands, palms up. "I mean, I can try. I just don't think it's possible to hack into a general's email."

"Are you saying you can't do it?" The velvet softness of Atwah's voice had a thread of steel to it. Rian sat forward. If Augie didn't give him the answer he wanted, Atwah would kill him. He had no regard for anyone's life but his own.

Atwah drew his gun and Rian's eyes darted to Augie's. *Do it*, she wanted to tell him. *Just do what he asks.*

"If you can't do it, then I have wasted my time and money. I have no other use for you." Atwah set the gun on the table and clicked his tongue. "I suppose I could sell you to someone else. Or kill you. Would you like to change your answer?"

Rian swallowed, her throat dry. She had to say something. "General Saleh's advisor has sent me to escort this man to the General himself. He is expecting us and will be very angry if anything happens to him." She forced herself to meet Atwah's eyes and hold them. Her stomach was twisting in fear, but she did not let her gaze drop.

Atwah's eyes narrowed as he stared at her. In one quick movement, he picked up the gun and pointed it at Rian's head. "What about you? Is the General expecting you? Or will you pay the price for this American's refusal?"

Pushing away from the table, Augie stood. "Hey, whoa,

everyone just relax. I'm happy to take a look at what you're asking and see if it's even doable. Just put the gun away."

Atwah held his position for a few more seconds, then finally put the gun in his side holster, keeping it within easy reach. Rian wanted to sag with relief but straightened her backbone instead. A quick glance at Atwah revealed a ghost of a smile as he looked at her. A sense of foreboding slid over her entire body. From Augie's quick reaction to defend her, he knew that Rian could be used as leverage over Augie. She had no doubt Atwah would exploit that as often as he could now. There was nothing else Augie could have done, though. Atwah would have killed both of them without even blinking.

Relaxed now that he was getting his way, Atwah pushed the laptop toward him, with a paper that had several lines of writing on it. Augie looked it all over before he began tapping at the keys. Everyone seemed focused on his fingers. The temperature in the room seemed to rise as he typed, and Rian felt a bead of sweat roll down her back. Her eyes were riveted to Augie's hands as well. They were nice hands, strong hands. He wasn't muscular like Omar or the guard, but he had a solid presence about him. She liked that.

Augie leaned forward, looking at the screen intently. His jaw clenched as he tapped away at the keyboard. He finally leaned back in his chair. "It's done." He glanced around the room, but his gaze stopped on her. One corner of his mouth lifted in a crooked half-smile, as if they'd done the assignment together and, in a way, they had. At least, they'd dealt with Atwah together. She had to admit, they'd made a good team so far.

Atwah pulled the laptop back toward him and started clicking into the General's private emails. Rian's stomach clenched as she watched a smile of satisfaction spread across his face. "The details we needed are right here." He sat back and looked at Omar. "Once the transfer of the oil terminal is complete, a tanker will be filled with oil and leave the port to symbolize the two governments working together. A great PR opportunity, it says." He gestured toward the email. "It is *definitely* an opportunity. One we will take full advantage of."

Omar laughed, and the sound grated on Rian's ears. What were they planning exactly?

"What should I do with them?" Omar asked, flicking his hand toward Rian and Augie.

"Take them to the cellar for now. We might have need of one or both of them later." Atwah was completely focused on the laptop and didn't even look up after he gave his orders.

One guard stayed in the room with Atwah, while Omar and the muscular guard took Augie and Rian down the hall and into another room. They removed a small rug from the floor that revealed a trap door. Tugging on it, Omar finally pried the door loose. The opening was barely big enough for an adult to get through.

"Surely you can provide better accommodations," Rian said, her lungs constricting at the thought of getting into such a small, dark space.

"We have our orders." The guard pushed her toward the opening.

Rian took a deep breath and was relieved to see a ladder on the side as she drew closer. Grabbing on, she climbed down. The area below wasn't as small of a space as she had imagined. It looked to have been a small wine cellar at one time, but now only boasted some wooden shelves and empty bags that looked like they'd been used for storing rice and beans. Augie hopped down beside her and Omar closed the door without a word. The only light was from the room above that filtered in around the edges of the door.

A small comfort, but one Rian held on to. She'd never liked complete darkness.

Augie touched her arm. She hadn't been expecting him to reach out, and she jumped a bit. He pulled his hand back immediately. "Hey, are you okay?"

She drew back and folded her arms to steady herself. "Of course."

Even though it was dark, she could feel his eyes on her. He finally stepped away, walking around the small room. He bent down occasionally to start stacking the empty cloth bags on the floor. When he'd gathered them all up, he walked over to the wooden shelves against the wall and pulled on them. They came away from the wall easily. Easing them to the floor, he began to pry the wood apart, grunting with the effort. With a crack, the wood began to give way, and soon he had the shelves in pieces on the floor. Augie separated out the longer boards that made up the shelves and arranged them on the ground. Putting a few of the cloth bags down on it, he turned toward her.

"I know it's not much, but at least we'll be off the ground." He sat down, but left plenty of space for her. "I think we need to talk."

Her eyes were adjusting to the dim light and his cross-legged shadow on the small pallet made him look like an ancient ruler on his throne. Allowing herself a small smile at the absurdity of that thought, she moved toward him. They *did* need to talk.

Nervousness overtook her at the conversation before them and she stumbled as she took the few steps to where he was sitting, nearly falling on him. He caught her and carefully lowered her down beside him on the floor. "Rian."

The moment was not lost on her. This was the first time someone who knew she was a woman had said her name out loud since her mother had died.

She pulled her knees up to her chest and hugged them. "How

did you find out?" Her voice was soft, as if she really didn't want to know the answer. But she did. She had to know.

"When you were sleeping in the camp, your keffiyeh slipped down to your shoulders. I noticed you have no Adam's apple, your skin is smooth, too smooth for a young man of your age, and," he cleared his throat. "um, well, you also have um, curves. I can't believe I didn't see it before."

"No one has seen it before." She turned to him and leaned in, wanting to stress the importance of what she was about to say. "And you cannot tell anyone. This is the only way for me to stay safe and be allowed to participate in our fight for freedom."

Augie frowned and looked away. "Of course I'll keep your secret. You don't have to worry about that."

She let out a sigh, not wanting to hurt his feelings or call his honor into question. But this was her life they were discussing. "You can't treat me any differently, now, or it will give me away. No one must even suspect I am anything other than a messenger boy for Malek."

"I understand." Augie's eyes met hers, the small shaft of light from above emphasizing his blue depths that asked her to trust him. She wanted to, but trust was something she had a hard time giving to anyone. "How long have you been living like this?"

"Since my mother died. I let everyone think I'd died along with her and then became a boy to protect myself. A girl alone on the streets of Benghazi . . ." She paused. "Well, it was very dangerous. But no one looks twice at a boy. Then I met Malek and joined the revolution, and my fate was sealed." She took a deep breath. Those had been difficult days, when she was still learning to act as a boy. Malek had been so patient. She'd told him she'd never had a father in her life to show her how to behave, and he'd taken her under his wing. She owed him so much for helping her find her place, even without knowing her secret. She'd always be grateful to him for that.

"What will happen when people start to question that you never grow older? You can't grow a beard." He nudged her shoulder and exhaled. "As much as you want to, you can't hide your true self forever. Do you have a plan for when those questions start being asked?"

"I will do it as long as I am able." She kept her bottom on the wood, but stretched her legs in front of her, comfortable with Augie's word that he wouldn't give her away. And while she rarely gave her trust to someone so easily, deep down she knew he wouldn't betray her. "You don't have to worry. I can take care of myself. You'd be surprised at the situations I've gotten myself out of."

"I have no doubt of that." Augie leaned back against the dirt wall, shifting around trying to find a comfortable spot. "And we might need your skills at getting out of situations sooner than we think."

"It won't be easy to get out of this one. Atwah definitely has a plan, but I think it's more than disrupting the peace talks." She glanced back at Augie. "After what happened upstairs, he's going to use me to force you to do whatever he has planned next, you know."

Augie leaned forward until their shoulders were nearly touching again. "Well, I have a little plan of my own. When Atwah wasn't looking, I was able to send Colt our location with the laptop. Hopefully the cavalry will be here before anything else like that happens."

Surprise jolted through her. "You did? But everyone was watching you."

He blew on his fingers, then buffed them on his shirt. "It's a gift. And I'm wearing my lucky shirt, so I can't go wrong."

Rian grinned. "Then I'm very grateful for your gift *and* your lucky shirt." She could feel warmth coming from his body behind her, and had to stop herself from leaning back into it. It was so tempting, though. The cold was starting to seep through her, and it would only get worse as the night wore on, though Augie's little pallet beneath them would really help to battle the cold.

Augie reached back and brought forward another cloth bag. "Here. Wrap this around your shoulders. We're going to need to conserve body heat as much as possible." He hesitated. "You know, even if you weren't a woman, we would still need to huddle together to get some warmth."

A faint flush had stained his cheeks, and Rian smiled. "Well, as long as you aren't giving me any preferential treatment." She wrapped the bag around her shoulders, then leaned into him. His arm came around her. "I hope our cavalry is already on their way. We're going to need some help to stop whatever Atwah is planning."

Augie rubbed her arm and warmth raced through her veins. How long had it been since anyone had held her? Hugged her with any sort of kindness or affection? She couldn't recall. But her body was awakening to feelings that had long been dormant or non-existent. A little part of her was scared to open that door, while the other part was telling her it was past time.

Augie was quiet, and for a moment, Rian wondered if he'd gone to sleep. "We've been chasing Atwah for a while now, and I've done a lot of research on him, trying to understand what makes him tick. From what I can tell, Atwah is only ever after one thing: power. He craves it. He wants to be feared and admired. He likes having people's lives in his hands. And he'll do anything he can to convert more people to his cause and have power over them. If he can get a foothold in Libya . . ." He stopped and exhaled a long breath. "Well, that's why we've got to stop him. No matter what."

Augie's words sounded ominous---especially when he was sitting with her in a cellar in near-darkness with Atwah upstairs. But Rian closed her eyes and nodded. No matter what they were in this together. They'd do whatever it took.

And hope they escaped with their lives.

CHAPTER SEVEN

Augie's arm was numb, but he didn't dare move it. Rian had finally fallen asleep, using his arm as a pillow. Sometime during the night, the light had been switched off in the room above them, plunging them into darkness. Now, though, a small beam of sunlight filtered through the trap door down to where they slept, but he had no way of knowing if it was morning or afternoon. They hadn't heard any movement upstairs yet, though, so it was probably morning.

He turned to look at the woman next to him. She looked so different in sleep. Carefree. Innocent. When she was awake, her eyes were wary, always watching, a tightness around her mouth as if she was constantly assessing the situation. Which she probably was, with a secret like hers.

How had she fooled so many for so long?

She'd obviously cut her hair and used her keffiyeh to cover her neck and lower face when she needed to. But this close, her softness and femininity were impossible to overlook. He brushed a bit of her short, uneven hair back from her forehead. Rian had told him in no uncertain terms that he couldn't treat her any differently or else he'd give her away. In this moment, however, with no one to witness, he couldn't help himself. He was drawn to her strength and fighting spirit and all the things he imagined she'd had to overcome to this point. He wanted to know everything about her.

She frowned in her sleep and began to slowly move her head from side to side, but she didn't wake. After a few more seconds, she began murmuring *'um, 'um*. Her body tensed, and the words grew louder. Augie recognized the Arabic word for *mother* and his hold on her tightened. Was she having a bad dream about her mother?

Rian opened her eyes, keeping herself very still as she got her bearings. Holding Augie's gaze for an extra moment, she sat up without a word and arranged her keffiyeh around her neck and shoulders. He sat up as well and flexed his arm, trying to bring feeling back into it.

She took a few deep breaths, then stood. Without even glancing back at him, she looked up at the trap door and rolled her neck, as if trying to get some kinks out. "Have you heard anything from upstairs?"

Augie shook his head, wincing as the little needles of pain flowing through his arm heralded the fact that feeling was returning. "Nope. All quiet."

Rian walked the perimeter of the small room, crouching down in one corner. She picked something up and brushed the dirt off, but Augie couldn't quite see what it was. She turned around with a grin on her face. "Look what I found."

Her smile lit up her whole face and Augie was mesmerized. The light in her deep, brown eyes warmed him as if he had just been given the best hot chocolate in the world on a cold morning. Inwardly shaking himself, he focused on what was in her hand. She held out two medium-sized, but somewhat shriveled, potatoes.

His stomach grumbled with hunger. How long had it been since they'd eaten that jerky? It seemed a lifetime ago.

Augie returned her grin and took the smaller of the potatoes. "You are a miracle worker."

He rubbed the potato on his pant leg, trying to get off as much dirt as possible. Biting down through the skin, he was surprised that it didn't taste bitter. He'd been preparing himself for that. Either it wasn't as old as he'd thought, or he was hungrier than he'd imagined. Chewing slowly, he watched as Rian sat back down next to him.

"You talk in your sleep," he said between bites, trying to keep his tone casual.

Rian finished chewing her bite and swallowed. She met his gaze, quickly hiding the worry shadowing her eyes. "What did I say?"

"You were calling out for your mother." Augie finished the last bite of his potato. He didn't want to press her if the memory of her mother's death was too hard. Doing that might damage the trust they'd built between them by making her feel uncomfortable. He swallowed. "You don't have to talk about it. I know your mother passed away during the war, but what about your father?"

She bit her lip and didn't speak for a few moments. Augie was about to say she didn't need to tell him if she didn't want to, when she started speaking. "My father was an American, actually. He was part of a diplomatic team at a U.S. mission in Benghazi. My mother helped with interpreting there sometimes. That's how they met. They fell in love and got married, and I arrived soon after. My father planned to take us all to America with him, but one morning, he left for work and never returned. My mother went to the consulate and was told he'd been evacuated, but that was all they could say. Protests started in Benghazi that exploded into an uprising, and war broke out soon after. My mother waited for him to come for her until the day she died."

Augie reached for her hand and squeezed her fingers. "I'm sorry." She'd spoken so quickly, as if she wanted to get it all out as fast as possible. It was easy to see the subject was still tender for her.

Rian lowered her eyes to the ground. "She was so sure he would come back for us, but I knew he wouldn't. He'd left his Libyan wife and daughter behind and hadn't looked back." She sighed.

Before Augie could say anything else, the trap door above them opened. Atwah's guard peered down at them. "Come," he said gruffly.

Rian stood and brushed off her hands. She went up first, and Augie followed close behind. He didn't want to let her out of his sight while they were being held hostage. Atwah and his men were too unpredictable---for men or women. They needed to stay together.

Once they were standing in the room above the cellar, the guard pointed toward a door. "Go in there and clean up. Then I will take you to Atwah." They trudged in the direction he'd pointed them to.

"He's a man of few words," Augie said with a quirk of his eyebrow. "I think he's starting to warm up to us, though."

Rian gave him a half-smile. "As long as the words he says include cleaning up, food, or water. That's what I want to hear." She walked into the bathroom first and closed the door. Augie leaned against the wall and took a look around. The house windows were small, but arched. There were few furnishings beyond a sofa and a few chairs. The hall leading to the front door didn't seem to be guarded at the moment. He took a step toward it to see if his theory was correct, but Atwah's guard appeared in the doorway.

He stood there, staring at Augie with his black eyes, his chest puffed out. "Hurry up."

Augie lifted his chin in acknowledgment. He heard the water in the bathroom turn off, and Rian opened the door. She glanced at the guard, then stepped out so they could trade places. He didn't like the guard watching over Rian while he was out of sight in the bathroom, but Augie assured himself he would be able to hear if the guy came any closer to her.

Rian let out a long breath and shook her head, as if she could read his thoughts. She leaned in close to his ear. "Remember."

He couldn't treat her differently. His mind knew it, but instinctively, he was having trouble with the concept. He'd have to try harder.

"Oh, don't worry about me, bro. I'm good." He said it loudly enough that the guard could hear, then focused on Rian and drew his eyebrows together. "Wait, do they say 'bro' in Libya? Should I use 'buddy' instead?"

Rian suppressed a smile and rolled her eyes as he closed the door. Thinking of her as a boy was nearly impossible now, but he was determined to do it. If he didn't, and someone found out, her deception would be looked at as a betrayal and he would have more or less signed her death warrant. He needed to keep that in the forefront of his mind.

Looking in the mirror, he rubbed his hand over the stubble on his chin. What he wouldn't give for a razor. Or a comb. He ran a hand through his hair, then splashed water over his face, trying to wash away some of the grime of the last few days. He'd never wanted a shower more than at that moment. Dust had found its way onto every square inch of him, and in some cases had covered those inches in several layers. But there was nothing he could do about it now.

Quickly using the facilities, he washed his hands and opened the door to rejoin Rian in the living room. The guard motioned for them to follow him down the hall. He took them back to the room they'd met in last night. When they entered, Augie noticed that Atwah was sitting in the same chair he'd been in last night. Had he even moved since they'd left him?

"Ahh, good morning," he said, his greeting more suited to a host with important guests. He waved his arm toward the other two chairs. "Sit down."

Rian and Augie retook their previous positions at the table, sitting next to each other and across from Atwah. A plate of oranges and sweet breads were in the middle of the table, as well as some turnovers to the side of it. Augie's mouth began to water at the sight of all the food.

Atwah followed his gaze and reached forward to push the plate toward him. "Eat, eat." He pointed to the turnover. "We have some *bureek* that is the best I've tasted, and you must be hungry. I'm sorry you weren't given more food yesterday, but war is difficult for everyone, and food is a privilege." He took one of the turnovers from the plate and bit into it, still watching Augie.

Augie barely resisted raising his eyebrows. What was Atwah trying to say? At least he knew the food wasn't poisoned, since Atwah was eating it as well. But Augie didn't ask any questions of their "host." He merely took two turnovers and reached back to hand one to Rian. She frowned, but took it. Augie winced inwardly. *Don't do anything for her. Treat her like another guy.*

Atwah pointed to his guard. "Fahad, water, please."

Fahad came forward with two bottles of water and set one next to Augie's elbow and the other near Rian. Augie was starting to get suspicious. Why were they being treated so nicely all of a sudden?

But Atwah didn't seem to notice anything amiss and leaned back in his chair. He looked directly at Rian. "I gather from our conversation yesterday that you are loyal to General Saleh and want to carry out his orders to deliver the American to him." He paused, but continued when Rian didn't respond. "I'm sure you've realized General Saleh's war efforts have been admirable, but he doesn't have the appeal to keep the loyalty of his men. That's why he's reaching out for this peace deal when he should be pushing forward to take Tripoli. It is only then that Libya can be united."

Rian stared at Atwah as if weighing her words. She pulled her keffiyeh closer around her shoulders, then inhaled deeply before she spoke. "The people are suffering and want this war to end. They want housing that isn't marked by bullets and bombs, food in the markets, and hope in the future. Peace talks and working toward democracy will give them that."

"*Oufft,*" Atwah said, looking annoyed. He dismissed her words with a wave of his hand. "I had hoped for more from you, but I see that you are nothing but a boy, yet. You don't know the dealings of adults and what is best for this country."

Rian stood so quickly her chair clattered to the floor behind her. She put her hands on the table and leaned toward Atwah. "I've fought this war my *entire* life. It's outsiders like you that don't understand Libya and her needs. The best thing for this country is to throw out the foreigners, including you, and let the citizens decide her leaders."

Augie stared at her. She was breathing hard, her face flushed, and her chin raised as she confronted one of the most dangerous men on the planet. She was unafraid and unapologetic.

A mix of awe and fear raced through him. What would Atwah do in the face of her defiance? She was so magnificent in that moment, standing tall and facing down her country's enemy. Augie would remember it for the rest of his life.

Atwah's eyes narrowed and his fists clenched, but he let out a low chuckle that sounded as if it came from the underbelly of a netherworld. "Soon you will see that *I* am what Libya needs. I am the one who will unite the people and bring this country back to the glorious power she once had." He turned to Augie. "And you are going to help me position myself."

Augie reluctantly tore his eyes away from Rian to look at Atwah. "What do you mean?" Now they were getting down to the real reason they'd been called here.

"General Saleh received an encoded message, and I need you to open it so I can see the contents. When that is finished, you will tell me how to encode a response in return, as if the message were coming from him." He stood and looked down at Augie. "You have one hour."

At that pronouncement, the door behind Atwah opened and Omar walked in. He spoke in low tones to their captor, reporting on the tanker being loaded. Was that what they were after? The symbolic tanker that would be loaded with oil and sail from the port to show the new partnership between General Saleh and the Prime Minister? The oil itself would be worth several million dollars on the black market, and with Atwah's funds being frozen, the money could help bankroll his organization for a few months. But this seemed a bit too elaborate for it to be just a money grab. Augie wasn't sure what to think.

"Get to work." Atwah told him before he moved to the door. He conversed quietly with Fahad and Omar and didn't seem to be keeping an eye on either of his prisoners. Augie glanced over at Rian who was staring at the three men. Maybe she could hear more of their conversation and get some information that could help them stop whatever Atwah was planning.

For now, though, he had a job to do. He bent to his task. General Saleh had several sequences in his security protocol to get through, and then Augie had to work on reverse engineering the encryption. It didn't take long for him to break it and read the encoded message. From what he could tell, the email to General Saleh was confirming the final details for the peace talks. They would be doing a small ceremonial handoff of the oil terminal at Ras Lanuf from General Saleh to the Prime Minister. Then the tanker would be allowed to leave the port laden with oil and show the world that Libya was back in the oil business.

The pieces were all starting to come together. Atwah had traveled to Ras Lanuf with busloads of soldiers that were meant to replace General Saleh's---men who were supposed to peacefully transition control of the oil field from the General to the Prime Minister. But Atwah had turned these soldiers to his cause somehow, tricked them into giving him their loyalty. And now Atwah needed the details of the peace talks because he was going to have the oil terminal turned over to him and his men instead of the Prime Minister. Atwah was preparing for battle and needed the details so he could launch a surprise attack. But how could Augie stop it?

Quickly looking to make sure Atwah was still speaking to the other two men, he started to send a code to Abby. Before he could finish and press send, however, Atwah was over his shoulder.

"Did you get the message decoded?" He leaned down and pulled the laptop toward him.

Augie yanked the laptop back, nearly coming out of his chair to get his finger on the delete button as fast as he could. Every muscle in his body was focused on deleting the evidence he'd tried to send a message. He held on as tight as he could and when he was sure there was nothing to link him to his attempt to contact Abby, he let it go. "There. Now I'm finished."

Atwah frowned and gave the laptop a thorough scan. Augie held his breath, but any evidence of the message had been deleted.

Atwah soon focused on the general's emails. "It's just as we thought." He turned to Omar, squaring his shoulders. "We need the men in position tonight."

Omar straightened his spine and looked like he was going to salute, but decided not to at the last minute. "We'll be ready. Every soldier is anxious to prove his loyalty to you."

"Now, can I send a message back to the Prime Minister's people and it will look like it came from Saleh?" Atwah asked Augie, still looking at the email in front of him.

"Yes." Augie reluctantly showed him how to do it. Atwah bent to the task.

Augie could just see over his shoulder as Atwah typed. The message said that due to security concerns, he was changing the location of the ceremony, but Augie couldn't see to where. When Atwah was finished, he pressed send and closed the laptop with a decisive snap. "Everything is in place."

Augie reached forward to the food plate and took another turnover. He also managed to palm an orange and slip that into the pocket of his cargo pants. Who knew when they would be offered food again?

Atwah called Fahad forward. "Take them back to the cellar."

Inwardly, Augie groaned. It was going to be a long day in the cellar then. But at least he would know they were safe for the moment. Hopefully Colt had gotten his location from the message he'd sent last night and the team was on their way.

As they passed Omar, Augie saw the gleam in his eyes and could feel battle anticipation rolling off of him, as if he was looking forward to what was to come. Augie kept his eyes straight ahead. He couldn't say the same.

The guard opened the trap door, and Rian went down the ladder first, then Augie. Once the opening was closed, Rian started pacing the room. On her second turn, she picked up one of the wooden slats from the broken shelves and turned it over and over in her hand. Rummaging through what was left of the shelves, she started using the slat she had in her hand to pound the nails from the remnants of the shelves.

"What are you doing?" Augie asked, moving closer. "You know, when I'm really stressed out, I recite Abel's binomial theorem to myself. But I guess pounding on wood could be a stress-reliever as well."

She drew her eyebrows together in confusion. "I'm not doing this for stress relief." She stopped and motioned to the wood she was holding. "I'm going to build a weapon. We've got to escape. You probably figured out that they're going to take over the terminal. We have to stop them, and we can't do it unarmed." She pounded harder and then held up the nail she'd gotten out. "If we get enough of these, we can put them in a pattern, like this." She held the nail to the wood to show him.

"You're making a nail-studded club." Augie shook his head in admiration. "That's brilliant."

She smiled and handed the nail to him. "Let's get this done. It's time for us to leave."

CHAPTER EIGHT

Having a nail-studded wooden club in her hand made Rian feel a little better. They weren't entirely helpless. It had taken some extra effort to pound the ancient, but still sharp, nails through the slat and make it into a weapon, but every minute had been worth it. Thankfully Atwah and his guards had been in another part of the house and hadn't heard any of their crude hammering.

Augie had collected all of the cloth bags and stuffed them into the corner. He'd shaped them into thirds, perhaps in an attempt to fool the guards---should they open the trap door---into thinking that they were huddled in the corner? Rian wasn't sure, but she didn't say anything.

When he was done he turned to look at her, his eyes going to the club she'd made. "Well, it definitely looks threatening and could scare someone off. But that's a close-quarters weapon. Do you think you'd be able to use it?"

"If I have to." Rian had been in a few situations over the years where having a weapon, and knowing how to use it, had saved her life. "I just want to be as prepared as I can."

Augie looked up at the trap door. "I haven't heard anyone for a while. Maybe now is our chance." He walked over to the ladder and climbed up until he could touch the bottom of the door. He pushed on it, and when it didn't budge, he pushed harder, trying to wedge himself between the wall and the door for leverage so he didn't fall.

The trap door inched open, so he pushed harder. When there was enough space, Augie carefully stuck his head out and didn't see anyone in the room. "Looks clear," he whispered down to her. He climbed through the door and waited for her to do the same. When they were both upstairs, he carefully closed the door and arranged the rug over it. "Let's go."

As they were creeping down the hall, every creak of the floor seemed amplified ten times over. Rian quickened her step. They needed to get outside.

A door opened behind them, and they moved around the corner in the living room nearest the front door. She took a breath and held it to try and quiet her thundering heart. She looked up at Augie. He seemed calm on the outside, but his jaw was clenched tight. At least he was good at hiding fear.

When no one came, and the house was quiet again, Rian moved to the window at the side of the room. It had a little bit bigger arch than normal windows, one they could fit through. They also would have a little cover in the shadows on the side of the house instead of being in full view of the front door. She unlatched the window sash and pushed the shutters back. She handed the club to Augie and climbed through the window, dropping easily to the ground. Augie was right behind her.

Rian pulled her keffiyeh around the lower half of her face. That would help her blend in, but there wasn't anything like that for

Augie. His red hair and pale complexion made him easy to spot, but their options were limited at the moment. She motioned toward the back of the house with her head. He nodded in acknowledgment and handed her club back.

Keeping low, they went to the back of the house and found a small alley behind the row houses. Staying in the shadows as much as possible, they headed away from the house Atwah was occupying and toward the entrance to the row housing where the bus had dropped them off yesterday.

"Where are we going exactly?" Augie said, his voice low.

"We need to steal a phone." Rian peered around a corner and kept walking. There was a small garden area up ahead that had a small stone wall and trees hanging low over the alley. Maybe he could hide there while she tried to blend in long enough to find a phone. "I want you to stay hidden while I scout things out in the houses on this row."

Augie touched her elbow to slow her step. "I think we should stay together. We've been a good team so far."

She stopped to face him. His blue eyes stared into hers, and she couldn't turn away. Didn't want to. She'd never seen eyes that were as blue as a summer sky. "I won't be gone long. I'm small and won't stand out like you will. I can slip into one of the houses where the soldiers keep their gear."

"What if you're caught?" Worry lines furrowed his brow and she wanted to reach up and smooth them away.

"If that happens, you'll be free to escape and alert Colt to what Atwah has planned." She shrugged her shoulders.

"I'm not going to wait here while you put yourself in harm's way." The muscle in his jaw worked, and his grip on her elbow tightened. "There's got to be a better plan."

"I'd like to hear it." She moved toward the tree overhang. It would probably be best if both of them were out of sight while they discussed this.

"We could find an office of some kind around here, I bet. A hotel. A store. Somewhere with a phone or a computer with internet." He ducked his head as they used the shelter of the tree to shield them from anyone who might be looking out a window.

Rian bit her lip. "The closest hotel is at least four kilometers away. I don't know if we could make it without being seen."

Augie stared at the house behind them. It looked just like the one they'd been held in, only smaller. "What if we borrowed one of the soldiers' keffiyehs? That could hide my hair and face long enough for us to make it to the hotel."

His face was so earnest, it was hard to say no to him. His plan did have possibilities and maybe it would be best to stay together. She glanced over her shoulder. "Yes. That could work. But you have to stay here while I go inside to get the keffiyeh."

Augie pressed his lips together, obviously not liking the separation, but not having a better idea. "Okay, on one condition. That you call out if you get in trouble."

"What would you do if I did?" She was genuinely curious.

"I'd come in and get you. Help you escape." His jaw was set. He was determined.

Having someone want to protect her like this was a foreign feeling, but it filled her full of warmth. He was so kind and considerate of her, but she had her secret to think about. "Just remember, you have to treat me like I was the young man you first met. Give me a chance to get out of any situations on my own. I've been taking care of myself for a very long time. Today is no different."

He took her hand, his brow furrowed. "It's different to me." He looked to the sky and inhaled a long breath, then faced her again. "Rian, I don't like playing games with your life. I can't stand by and watch you fight alone. I'm sorry. I will keep your secret, but I don't want to see you hurt."

"But I've fought before you got here, and I'll do it again after you leave." Her hand felt right in his, but she pulled away. Her feelings at having someone care so much about her well-being was confusing, and she wasn't sure how to react. "Just call me 'bro,' tell me you're good, and I'll go get you a keffiyeh. Then we'll get to the hotel and call Captain Mitchell."

He put his hands in his pants pocket and gave her a crooked smile. "Okay, bro, I'm good."

She grinned back at him and started toward the house. Lightly running across the small courtyard, she flattened herself against the side of the house. Peeking in the first window, she could see the four soldiers in the kitchen eating. Perfect. The front of the house would be empty. With one more glance back at Augie who watched her from underneath the tree, she moved to the window nearest the front door. Silently opening the shutters, she hoisted herself up and in.

The men's gear was ready and waiting near the front door and Rian crept forward, rummaging through the first bag until she found a keffiyeh. Snatching it up, she was about to go back the way she'd come when she saw a cell phone on the table. It was small and brick-like, obviously not an up-to-date new phone, but it would work for a call. Taking a small detour, she took the phone and nearly leapt out the window. Her heart was pounding so hard that she could feel the blood roaring in her ears. Once her feet touched the ground next to the house, she slowly closed the shutters and headed back to where Augie was waiting.

He breathed a sigh of relief when she reached him. She handed him the keffiyeh and as he started to put it on, she pulled out the cell phone. "Look what I got."

His eyes widened. "That will save us a trip to the hotel."

She handed it to him, and he punched in a long string of numbers. He put it to his ear. "Colt, it's Augie." He smiled. "I'm glad you got it. Did you track it? Okay." He paused to listen and Rian leaned in, wishing she could hear what Colt was saying, too.

"Yeah, we confirmed Atwah's presence at the camp, and were about to leave when we were taken here." Augie blew out a breath. "I know. Where can we meet? We need to get to you. Atwah is---"

Augie was slammed to the ground and the phone knocked out of his hand. Omar landed on top of him with his gun to Augie's head. "You will pay for this." He glanced at Rian who had stumbled backward a few feet. "You should have stayed where you were."

Rian's heart dropped to her toes. How had they not heard him coming? They'd been too caught up in staying hidden from the soldiers in the house, they'd missed the danger in the alley. "Omar, don't do this. You're more than Atwah's stooge. Let us go."

Omar got to his feet with a sneer on his face. Augie stood, brushing off his pants before he straightened. Omar kept the gun pointed at Augie's torso. "What do you know of it? Atwah has promised me a place in his army at his side. Once his plan is in motion, Libya will look to us for leadership." His chest puffed out a bit. "I've been preparing my whole life for this opportunity."

The more he talked, the more he lowered his gun. Rian stepped a bit closer. "I heard once that you were stolen as a child and raised for war. If Atwah is put in charge, he will do that to other boys. He will use anyone and everyone for his own gain. Do you want that? Do you want others to suffer as you have?"

Omar's eyebrows drew together, and he frowned. "I learned what I needed to learn to survive. If Atwah feels it's necessary to raise the next generation to be warriors, then they will learn that, too. Life as a trained soldier is necessary to control a country and make her a world power."

"If you turn us over to Atwah, he will kill us." Augie angled his head to look at Omar. "Let us go. Do the honorable thing."

"What do you know of honor?" He spit on the ground. "I will do what's best for me."

"It doesn't have to be that way." Rian leaned towards him, her tone urgent. "You could join us. You've worked with Malek. You know what we're fighting for. Commit to the cause. Our people need peace, not whatever Atwah has planned. Deep in your heart, you know that." Her hands clasped together as if in a silent plea.

Omar lowered the gun and ran a hand over his face with a grunt. "You know I revere Omar al-Mukhtar, the hero of Libya who fought for the resistance. He was a great man."

Rian could feel him wavering, and hope soared in her heart. "Omar al-Mukhtar defended Libya's freedom and sacrificed everything to that end. He never let his own interests come before the country."

Omar lowered his chin as if to reverence his hero. "He was a warrior like no other."

"You share a name. You could share a legacy," Augie put in. "Tell us what Atwah is planning so we can stop it. Fight for the people, not the man who wants to oppress them."

Omar hung his head and stepped back. "There is more than you think. Atwah is going to---"

But before he could finish Fahad appeared at the end of the alley. He spotted them and shouted, "There they are!"

Omar raised his gun to Augie's head, his expression hardening. "War is hard for everyone and choices must be made," he murmured. "I really am sorry."

"You should be," Augie said, as they all watched Fahad jog toward their position.

Fahad reached them with two other guards. He grabbed Rian's

arm and shook her until her teeth rattled in her head. "You will be lucky to live until the sun sets," he snarled.

Rian could barely contain her wince and tried to adjust her position so her arm wasn't being twisted. She didn't say anything. What was there to say? They were caught.

Facing Augie, he caught her attention with his widened eyes returning to the ground at his feet, then looking back up at her. When she looked down, she saw her nail-studded club lying there. She tried to shake her head, to tell him not to do whatever he was planning, but he dropped to the ground and came back up swinging. The club hit Fahad in the shoulder. He reeled back.

"Run!" Augie shouted as he turned on his heel and took off.

Rian yanked her arm out of Fahad's grasp. She darted after Augie, weaving back and forth in case Omar decided to shoot. They were nearly to the end of the alley. Once they got clear, they might be able to disappear in the town somewhere. She heard Augie's breaths coming hard as they ran side by side. She put on a burst of speed, but slowed down when four soldiers blocked the alley exit.

She stopped and looked to the side and behind them. Soldiers in every house. Fahad and Omar nearly on top of them. They were trapped. She bent over and put her hands on her knees, her chest heaving as she breathed in and out through her mouth. "Using the club was risky. We gave it a good effort, though," she said to Augie, straightening.

"We did." He stood next to her, nearly shoulder-to-shoulder and they waited for Fahad and Omar. At least they knew that no matter what happened, they'd done all they could to escape.

Fahad ground his boots into the gravel, and as soon as the guard got close, didn't hesitate to shove Augie to the ground. His shirt was torn, and his shoulder bleeding. Augie calmly stood up and brushed off his pants and shirt. Rian was glad he hadn't antagonized the guard with a comment or by striking back. Fahad was angry and unpredictable.

"I won't even wait for Atwah to kill you," Fahad yelled, spittle flying out of his mouth. "I'll kill you for that myself."

Rian didn't doubt Fahad's word, but hopefully they could stall long enough for Colt and Malek to get here. She'd always said if she had to forfeit her life for Libya and her freedom, it will have been a life well spent. But as she marched through the alley with Augie at her side, she wasn't sure that was true anymore. Augie had made her think of future possibilities. Of things she'd never dared to let herself dream about before. Having someone know her secret, who cared about her and her safety, made her think she might want to stop living a lie. To be herself.

But when she felt Omar's gun at her back, she crashed back to reality. She was probably marching to her death.

She felt Augie's eyes on her and turned to meet his gaze. If this was the end, she was glad he was there with her. Selfishly, she wished they had more time. More time to get to know him, to explore the feelings he evoked in her.

He gave her his crooked grin, and she returned it.

"You okay, bro?" he asked with a gleam in his eye.

"I'm good." And even with what was in front of them, she was. No matter what happened, it would be worth the sacrifice.

CHAPTER NINE

Fahad and Omar brought them back to the same room they'd been in that morning, where they'd eaten turnovers and oranges and hacked into General Saleh's email. The table was bare now, and Atwah was pacing the length of the room, his hands clenched at his sides. He stopped short when they came in and turned to face them. His eyes were as cold as Arctic ice, but their depths were full of white-hot rage.

Augie licked his lips and nervously draped the keffiyeh Rian had "borrowed" for him around his shoulders. If he was going to die, he wanted to be wearing it. She'd put herself in danger to help him hide his identity, and he would never forget it.

Atwah walked over and got very close to Augie's face. "Who did you call?" His words were clipped and demanding. "We can't reconnect to the number you dialed."

"I wasn't able to call anyone. Omar found us before I could." Augie took a step back, but managed to meet the terrorist's black gaze.

With barely a blink, Atwah shoved him hard against the wall.

The force of it knocked the breath out of Augie, but before he could react, Atwah's hands were around his neck, squeezing. "You're lying. Omar heard you speaking to someone."

Augie's throat was closed off, his lungs aching for air. He opened his mouth, but nothing came out. He put his hand over Atwah's trying to pry his fingers off.

Darkness hovered at the edge of his vision, and Augie knew he was going to pass out. Atwah must have realized this as well and relaxed his hand just enough so that Augie could breathe. He gulped in air and tried to speak. "Okay, okay. I . . . I was trying to get hold of my boss, but the secretary said he wasn't there. I could only leave a message."

Atwah let go, and Augie slumped against the wall, holding his throat. His windpipe felt ten sizes too small for even a breath, and he was gasping. He bent over and tried to breathe in small incre- · ments, but all he could do was cough.

"Maybe your friend will tell me."

The words made Augie's blood run cold. He looked up in time to see Atwah push Rian to the wall, his hand easily circling her neck.

"No," Augie rasped out. "I'm telling you the truth."

"Who is your boss?" Atwah's voice was calm, as if they were discussing the weather and not holding someone's very life in his hand.

Rian's face was turning red, and she made a choking noise as Atwah squeezed harder.

"I work for a cybersecurity firm called BlackNet." Augie tried to remember all the details of the cover story he and Abby had made before this all began. "They were going to pay my ransom." Rian's eyes were wide, and for the first time since he'd met her, he could see fear on her face. He tried to move to her side, to help her, but Fahad held him back. "That's all I was doing. I just want my boss to pay my ransom so I can get out of here."

Fahad's grip on his arm was like a vise and he watched as Atwah squeezed Rian's neck even harder. She closed her eyes. Augie had never felt more desperate. "I'm telling the truth!" he shouted.

Atwah let go, and Rian fell to the ground. Fahad's grip loosened, and Augie shook him off, kneeling on the floor next to Rian. She was coughing, and though he wanted to hug her and make sure she was okay, he awkwardly patted her back instead.

"You're okay, man. You're okay." His words sounded so inadequate, but that was the only thing running through his mind. She was okay. She had to be.

Atwah stood next to them, rubbing his wrist while staring at them. "I treated you well, and you repaid me by trying to escape. There must be a punishment, so you'll remember your place in the future."

Augie shook his head at that pronouncement. Everyone who dealt with Atwah knew his punishments involved torture that almost always ended in death. His stomach twisted. He couldn't bear to watch Rian be hurt. "We'll remember. That won't happen again."

"No, it won't." Atwah motioned to Fahad. "Bring me the whip."

Fear and apprehension flowed through Augie's body, his heart pounding painfully against his chest. He'd read all of Atwah's files. This was a man who enjoyed inflicting pain on others. Many of his victims were permanently maimed and scarred if they lived through the ordeal.

"That's not necessary." His voice was little more than a croak.

Rian tried to clear her throat and raised watery eyes to Augie. For just a moment, he saw sadness and regret before she shuttered her emotions. "We'll get through this," she whispered to him.

But would they? Another surge of adrenaline added to the fear already shooting through him.

Fahad left the room, but quickly returned with a cat o'nine tails. The whip was small and black, just like Atwah's eyes.

Oh, this was going to be ten times worse than he thought. Augie held up his shaking hands. What could he say to stop this from happening? "Hey, you know, this isn't going to work for me. I can't even handle dental work without having the laughing gas to help with the pain." He tipped his head toward the whip. "That looks pretty painful, and I don't see any laughing gas here, so can we just draw up a contract or something? I promise I won't run again. Please."

Atwah took the handle of the cat o'nine tails and tossed it from hand to hand, as if testing his grip. "I don't know what *laughing gas* is, but I know you won't be laughing when I am through with you."

The door opened and Omar came in, standing nearly at attention next to Fahad. If only he'd let them go when they had a chance. Augie stood. He inhaled and squared his shoulders. They were outnumbered, and there was no chance of escape. He was going to have to face what was coming. Augie was determined to do it with as much courage as he could muster.

Fahad stepped forward and showed Atwah his bloody shoulder. "This is the scar I will bear for the rest of my life. I'd like the American to bear a scar at my hand as well."

Atwah dipped his chin as if he were a king granting a request for a boon. "You will have your chance." The whip twitched in his hand, as if it was anxious to get started. "Bare them to the waist."

No. Augie stood in front of Rian, wanting to shield her, wishing she'd immediately left him behind and saved herself the moment Omar had appeared in that alley. "Escaping was my idea, I just dragged him along. He's just a boy. I'll take the whipping meant for him." He heard Rian's small intake of breath behind him, but he wasn't about to let this happen. Atwah could not discover Rian's secret. He would kill her where she stood.

"You would take the lashes meant for him?" Atwah raised his eyebrows. "Twenty lashes for you and twenty lashes more for your friend?"

Augie didn't hesitate. "Yes." Hope flickered through Augie at Atwah's words. If he would allow Augie to take Rian's lashes, her secret would be safe.

The whip shifted from hand to hand while Atwah mulled over Augie's proposal. "What does this boy mean to you?"

That was an impossible question for Augie to answer at the moment. Rian was starting to mean more to him than he'd ever thought possible, but of course he couldn't say that. "He's just a boy," Augie finally said.

Atwah pursed his lips and looked between Rian and Augie. Waiting for the verdict was excruciating, but Augie tried to hold in any emotions.

In the end, Atwah shook his head. "An admirable offer, but I can't allow it. You will both be punished." He flicked his hand and Fahad grabbed Augie's arm, twisting it until he was face-first against the wall. Rian soon joined him, her cheek smashed against the wall, her face turned to his.

"I'm sorry," he said softly to her.

She nodded and gave him a sad smile. "It's going to be okay."

But he knew it wouldn't be.

Augie tapped his forehead against the wall. He'd never felt so helpless. Anger flooded over him at the injustice of it all. "Don't do this!" he shouted to the men behind him. "You don't need to do this!"

Fahad grabbed the material of his shirt, and Augie's heart rate kicked up a notch.

"This is my lucky plaid shirt," Augie told him, twisting around to try to see Fahad. "Don't touch it."

"It's not very lucky for you," Fahad said, and ripped it halfway down the back. It tore in two like paper.

Omar allowed Rian to take off her keffiyeh and vest. The items dropped to the floor. She presented her back to him and he leaned forward to rip her shirt just like Fahad had done to Augie.

"Don't do this, Omar," Augie pleaded, his voice low. "If you have any honor at all, don't do this. I'm begging you."

Omar didn't look at him, just started to rip the material. When he made it halfway down Rian's back, though, he stopped. His eyes shot to Augie's.

"What's the problem?" Atwah said, moving forward to look over Omar's shoulder. He stared at Rian's back, her bindings clearly visible. Taking her arm, Atwah spun her around and looked her up and down with a sneer. "You are a woman."

"Yes." Her one-word answer was clear and defiant as she stood in front of the men in the room. "I am a woman," she repeated, lifting her chin to meet Atwah's eyes.

Atwah slapped her face and she fell to the floor, barely missing hitting her head on the corner of the table. "You shame us all with your deceit." He spit on the floor near where she'd fallen.

"Hey!" Augie shoved Atwah away from her and bent to help her up, but Fahad punched him in the side of the head. The room spun crazily and it was all Augie could do to stay standing.

Rian held her face and stood up on her own.

Atwah rubbed his hand over his beard, glaring at her. His gaze flicked to Augie. "A corrupt American and a lying, deceitful woman." He paused and glanced at Omar. "Neither of them deserves to live, but we can use them."

"How?" Omar's voice wasn't as sure as it had been. Was he having second thoughts about what he'd done? Augie hoped so.

"I will use them as examples to the men. They will see that our enemies will be shown no mercy." Atwah put the whip on the table. "Perhaps we will also show the General's men what will happen if they don't join us."

Fahad nodded, but Augie noticed Omar didn't seem to be as eager as before.

"What do we do with them until we move into position around the terminal?" Fahad asked, rubbing the knuckles of his hand as if he wanted to punch Augie again.

"Put them back into the cellar---and lock the door this time," Atwah ordered. "They've already cost me valuable time in making sure all is ready for tonight."

Augie leaned against the wall and briefly closed his eyes. The cellar sounded like a haven right now. He wanted to be anywhere other than this room. Fahad took him by the shoulder and shoved him toward the door. Augie grabbed his keffiyeh and made sure Rian was right behind him.

Coming back to the room with the cellar and going down the ladder was starting to feel like second nature now, even though it had been less than twenty-four hours since they'd first been held there. And now it would be the holding room while they awaited their punishment and, mostly likely, death. The whole situation was like a nightmare that played over and over in his mind.

He climbed down and stood at the bottom of the ladder waiting for Rian. When she was beside him, they both stood and watched while the trap door was shut. Then they heard the click of a padlock through the hasp. There was no escaping now.

Augie had a painful headache from the punch he'd taken. He reached out and touched Rian's forearm. "Are you okay?"

She sucked in a deep breath. "Not really." She took two steps to the wooden shelf that was still on the ground where Augie had placed it to protect them from the cold. She sank down. Pulling up her knees, she leaned over and covered her face with her hands.

Augie sat beside her and put his arm around her. She'd been able to put her vest on before they'd left the room to cover the rip in the back of her shirt, but her keffiyeh was gone. It seemed strange to see her hair uncovered.

He tucked her close to his side. "I'm sorry."

She leaned her head into his shoulder. "Would you really have taken my lashes for me?" Her voice was small and a thread of disbelief ran through her tone.

A little piece of his heart broke that she even had to ask the question. "Rian, I would have gladly taken your whipping. I never wanted your secret to come out." He lightly rubbed her back. "I was so scared for you. For us."

"Me, too," she whispered.

He felt a drip of wetness on his shirt and turned slightly so he could see her face. "Don't cry. It's not over yet. Colt knows where we are. He's on his way. We just have to be patient."

A sob escaped, and she buried her face in his shoulder. He let her cry, moving his hand in a slow circle on her back. "Shh, I'm here. We're going to get through this," he said, wanting to say something that would help, but not knowing what.

Her soft sobs went on for several minutes and Augie wished he could take her pain away. She'd risked so much. It couldn't end like this for her.

When her tears were spent, she sniffed softly. "I haven't cried like that since my mother died."

"Maybe you needed to." He resumed the soft circles on her back. "I'm a really good listener if you want to talk."

She took a shuddering breath. "I've only had myself to rely on for so long. Malek has been a protector of sorts, but we all look out for ourselves and what's best for the General." She leaned back to look at him, her eyes still wet from her tears. "No one has ever done something like that for me. Offered to sacrifice themselves to save me. Why would you do that? You hardly know me."

"How could I not? You're amazing with all you've done to survive and how you've carried your secret for so long. You deserve so much more than what you've had." He gently lifted her chin with one finger and ran his thumb over the tracks her tears had left on her face. "You amaze me. Your courage, your ingenuity. I've never met anyone like you." He looked down into her dark chocolate eyes and electricity arced between them. "Rian, I've . . . well, I've never kissed anyone before, but would you mind if I kissed you?"

He heard her soft intake of breath, and her entire body seemed to still. "I've never kissed anyone before, either." She nodded, as if to herself as much as to Augie. "Yes, I'd like you to kiss me."

He pivoted to face her. Her eyes widened as he reached up and slowly slid his palm across her cheek. Her skin was so soft, like warm silk under his fingers. He shifted forward, giving her plenty of time to change her mind. She watched him carefully, as if waiting for a signal of what came next. He gave her a small smile, wanting to put her at ease. Pushing his nervousness away, he moved his hand to the nape of her neck and cradled her head as he gently pulled her into his arms.

The first touch of his mouth to hers was featherlight, like a whisper shared between them. Augie closed his eyes, grateful he hadn't missed her lips. He gathered her closer to his body. Kissing her felt like coming home, as if he was always meant to be with her like this. Her hands circled his neck and tentatively trailed up through his hair, her touch sending tingles of warmth all the way down his spine. He tilted her head and deepened the kiss, not wanting it to ever end. The darkness enveloped them like a sweet refuge from the world, as if they were the only two people who existed and this kiss was all that mattered.

His heart was nearly pounding out of his chest when he reluctantly pulled back, resting his forehead on hers.

Her eyes were still closed, her breaths coming in fast puffs. "Augie."

His name on her lips sent another surge of warmth through him. Augie hugged her close. He hadn't planned to kiss her, but he didn't regret it. There was a fifty-fifty chance they were going to die if Colt didn't find them soon. And kissing Rian would be a sweet memory to carry him through to the end.

CHAPTER TEN

R ian glanced upward at the sound of footsteps overhead. Was Atwah preparing to leave? There was no way to tell. All they could do was wait, though she didn't mind as long as she was with Augie. Her mind replayed everything that had happened since this mission started. Her life as a boy was over. She'd never dreamed it would end this way. Whenever she'd thought of what could happen if she was ever discovered, she'd always thought it would come on her terms—that she would be the one to reveal herself somehow. But as soon as she'd seen the whip in Atwah's hand, she'd known it was over.

And that he wouldn't let her live.

She let out a small sigh. Hearing Augie say he'd gladly take the lashes meant for her, had tilted her world on its axis. She'd never had anyone offer to do anything like that for her before. In her world, everyone fended for themselves. But he'd offered to take the pain for her so she wouldn't be revealed. And then when she'd cried in front of him, he hadn't commented on her weakness, only told her she was amazing. Rian let her fingers touch her lips. After that declaration, he'd kissed her. She'd never really thought about kissing or realized what she'd been missing. Heat had raced through her veins the moment he'd asked if he could.

And she wanted to do it again.

She pressed her ear closer to his heart and his arm tightened around her. Right here in this moment, she felt safe. They were in a cold cellar, being held hostage by a terrorist who probably planned to kill them in the morning, but Rian was secure in Augie's embrace. It was strange, but was just so right.

"You asleep?" he asked, his voice rumbling through his chest underneath her ear.

"No." She lifted her head. "I've got too much going through my mind to sleep."

"Yeah, me too." His hand rubbed her shoulder, sending warmth along her arm. "When I'm on a stakeout with Griffin Force, and we know it's going to be a long one, I like to play this game." He paused, and though it was dark, Rian could tell he was grinning.

"What sort of game can we play in a cellar with very little light?" She tilted her head. "Even if you've been hiding dice or cards, we wouldn't be able to see them."

"It's called, 'What's the weirdest thing.' The more Augie spoke, the more he warmed to the subject. He obviously enjoyed this game. "So, it goes like this. I ask you a question like, what's the weirdest thing you've ever eaten? Or what's the weirdest thing you've ever bought, or the weirdest place you've ever visited? Things like that. Then you answer and then I see if I can top what you said."

"So we win if we're crowned the weirdest person?" Rian suppressed a smile. "Have you ever had a champion for this game?"

He barked a laugh. "Okay, I thought I was the aspiring comedian here, but come to think of it, I do win quite a bit at this game."

Rian chuckled at how surprised he sounded. "So, should I

answer the first question, then, the weirdest thing I've eaten?" He nodded and she thought about weird things she'd eaten for a long moment. "I think the weirdest thing I've ever eaten was *ma'danous*." She put her chin on his chest and wrinkled her nose. "It's like an herbal sausage. Lamb intestines stuffed with liver, kidney, lungs, rice, and herbs."

Augie's face was mostly in shadow, but she could see that he'd raised his eyebrows. "Wow. That's going to be hard to top." He tilted his head back against the wall. "Hmm... The weirdest thing I've ever eaten was when I was in Tel Aviv and ate a chocolate-covered locust. It was . . . crunchy." He gave her a low laugh. "I definitely think you win in the weird food department."

She glanced up at him, a bit surprised at how much she was enjoying herself despite their circumstances. "So now it's my turn to ask a question?" He nodded. "What is the weirdest thing you've ever . . . seen?"

"That would have to be the catacombs in Paris with millions of skeletal remains in them. Not necessarily weird, but definitely creepy." His hand squeezed her shoulder as he peered down at her in the low light. "What about you?"

"When my mother took me to the Roman ruins outside of Benghazi, there was a stone statue there, a strange face carved on the sun. The statue looked quite real and I thought the eyes followed me wherever I went." She bit her lip. "I was scared to sleep for many nights afterward, sure that the statue had followed us home and still watched me. My mother had to come into my room and sing to me." She'd locked all her memories of her mother away, believing that it would hurt too much to think about her, but here with Augie, the memory of her voice brought a smile to her face.

"What song did she sing?" Augie stroked her hair and Rian closed her eyes.

"A lullaby my father used to sing, actually." She began to hum the tune. "I remember it was about sunshine."

"Did it go like this? *You are my sunshine, my only sunshine, you make me happy, when skies are gray,*" he sang the words softly, but his voice reminded her vaguely of her father and how he'd tucked her safely into bed while he sang.

"Yes, that's it!" She sat up, awash with the memory of it. "My father used to sing it to me before I went to sleep. I loved hearing his voice." How had she forgotten?

"Well, I can see why he thought of gray skies. When I first got to Libya, everything seemed gray." Augie straightened, too, and rolled his neck from side to side, rubbing the muscles there. "Now that I've been here longer, I can see how wrong I was. It's mostly brown."

Rian playfully tapped his arm. "Now who's the comedian?" But she moved to sit beside him, her back against the wall. "There is so much more to Libya than gray and brown. I wish I could show you more. That we could visit the seashore, and I could show you the blue of the Mediterranean. You've never seen anything like it. It's the most beautiful blue in the world."

He held up his hands in mock surrender. "Oh, I believe you."

She was about to invite him to ask her another question, but all of the lightheartedness between them evaporated when the lock on the trap door was undone and the door opened. They moved apart just as Fahad stuck his head in. "Time to go."

Rian took a deep breath. This was it. Augie kissed her forehead, then got to his feet. He climbed the ladder quickly and reached back to help her out. Fahad was armed and enjoyed grinding his gun into Augie's side as he marched them through the house and out the front door. The buses were being loaded with soldiers again, and Rian and Augie were put in the front this time, next to the driver. Fahad sat next to Augie, but kept his eye on Rian, as if he was afraid she would try to run. But she knew better than to try. Besides, she wouldn't leave Augie on his own. Her fate was sealed now.

A few of the soldiers looked at her curiously, and she wished she still had her keffiyeh. At least none of them spoke to her. The buses rumbled to life and headed toward the oil terminal. Dusk was not far away, but the road was busy for this time of day. The closer the bus got to the oil terminal, the more pickup trucks they saw with anti-aircraft weapons in the back. Men stood on the side of the road holding AK-47s, watching them pass. Did they know what was about to happen? How many soldiers had been bribed or swayed by Atwah? Did the General or the Prime Minister have any men still loyal to them?

The bus they were riding in jolted to a stop before they'd reached the entrance to the terminal and Rian looked around in confusion. Why would they stop here? No one asked any questions, and the soldiers all stood and slowly filed off, joining the men from the three other buses behind them. Fahad waited until the seats were empty, then waved his gun to signal to her and Augie to get up. "It's time."

Rian exited first, with Augie behind her, then Fahad. The sun hung low in the sky. They probably had four hours left of daylight. She passed the men from their bus who were now lining up into a formation, as if they were getting ready to march in a parade. Fahad led her and Augie to the side of the crowd and they stood there with everyone else, waiting to see what happened next.

Atwah strode to the front and gracefully hopped up into the back of a pickup truck and stood next to the anti-aircraft gun. Surveying the crowd, he lifted his hands toward them. The entire scene looked staged, as if he were posing for the cover of a propaganda magazine.

"Today, you have pledged your loyalty to me and we will rise to meet our destiny. We will do what others have failed to accomplish. We will take the first step to showing the world what our capabilities are and drive the infidels to their knees. They will shrink and bow before the power that Libya wields." His voice rang out over their group, getting louder with each sentence. "We will stand against our enemies and together transform Libya from chaos to order. Sacrifices will be made today, but if we die, we will die as heroes. Libya will never forget this day!"

The crowd cheered as Atwah lifted his arms and pumped his fists. He was completely in his element, enjoying the adulation of the moment. Rian folded her arms and held them tightly against her.

"The time has come," Atwah shouted. "Let us go to take our places and make history."

He jumped down and led the small army as they marched toward the oil terminal. Fahad pushed Rian forward, hurrying her along, as if he didn't want to miss a moment of their arrival to whatever Atwah had planned next. Augie stayed by her side as they marched on the edge of the formation of soldiers.

The dust began to fill the air, and Rian reached for her keffiyeh to help keep the small particles out of her face, but again, the material she'd relied on wasn't there. It was so strange not to have it. Augie looked over at her, then reached up and took off the keffiyeh she'd gotten for him. He gave her his crooked half grin and handed it to her. As she put it on, she couldn't help but smile to herself. Augie had been the bright spot through this entire ordeal. And though it was all coming to an end, for just a moment, she wished she could kiss him one more time, to feel the security of being in his arms.

They crested a small hill, and the buildings and storage tanks of the oil terminal came into view. A large crowd stood near the gate. Were those General Saleh's troops, thinking they were only there to ceremonially hand over control to the Prime Minister? But as she got closer, Rian could make out several men in traditional clothing in the front, and a few more wearing suits beside them. They quietly waited with several dozen soldiers nearby.

She glanced at Augie, and his eyes were riveted to the scene in front of them as well.

"Malek," he said softly. His wide grin was filled with relief as he turned to her. "That has to mean Colt found us. They're here."

Rian stared harder at the crowd, trying to make out individual faces. He was right. There in the middle she could see Malek's familiar form and the general was next to him. They were ready for Atwah. All was not lost.

Atwah led his soldiers close to the gate, then held up his hand. The air was charged as the two groups eyed each other. Atwah snapped his fingers, and Fahad took her arm. Omar appeared at Augie's side and waved his gun toward the front where Atwah stood waiting. "Let's go."

The four of them started forward. Rian's pulse began to pound as they reached the front. With only a few steps to go until she reached Atwah, she was thrown to the ground at his feet.

"Kneel," Fahad commanded. Augie soon joined her with Omar's gun pressed into the side of his head.

When Rian was kneeling, Atwah called Fahad forward, his eyes darting to the gate. "They knew we were coming, which proves your theory that the woman, and American, were working for our enemies all along and alerted them. But our plan will still go forward. You will have the honor of showing everyone how we deal with those who betray us."

Fahad nodded and took his gun from the holster at his side. "Yes, *padrone.*"

Atwah walked a few steps away to the empty middle ground

between them and the group at the gate. The General and Malek stood watching, along with all of the soldiers surrounding them.

Everyone was silent, and all eyes were on Atwah. Not even a breeze ruffled the dust on the ground. It was as if even nature waited to hear what he would say.

"Our enemies are all around us, even in our very midst." He pointed to Rian, and Fahad tore the keffiyeh from her head and threw it on the ground. "A woman in our ranks, masquerading as a man, betrayed our honorable men with her deceitful ways."

Fahad put his gun to her head, and Rian closed her eyes. Adrenaline rushed through her. Was this the moment she would die? She wished she could have told Malek how much she'd appreciated him and what he'd done to protect her. How grateful she was that he'd given her a place in the fight for freedom. She wished she had one more moment with Augie, to thank him for allowing her to dream of something more for her future. But she didn't, and wishing wouldn't do any good.

The shot didn't come. Atwah droned on about her "betrayal" and how she should have done her duty in the home. She held in her snort of derision at his words. There hadn't *been* a home for her after her mother died, and she wasn't ashamed of what she'd done to survive. Rian raised her head to look at the men surrounding her. She'd always known it could end like this, but hoped it wouldn't. She lifted her chin another inch. She would not cower.

Atwah waved toward Augie with a flourish. "This woman has also conspired with an enemy and brought him here to undermine our authority. Today I will show you how we deal with our enemies both at home and abroad."

Rian reached out and took Augie's hand. He looked her in the eyes and then squeezed her fingers. Having him be the last person she looked at before she died was comforting. He had such a noble face. He wasn't handsome in a classical sense, his red hair and freckled nose making him stand out in a crowd, but it was his strong jaw and eyes that saw into her soul that made him handsome to her.

Atwah pulled his gun out and pointed it at Rian. A murmur went through the crowd and Rian could hear someone yelling from near the gate. A megaphone sounded, and the General began speaking through it.

"My people, only a coward kills an unarmed woman. We don't need any more killing. We need everyone to fight for freedom. Every man and every woman. Don't be fooled by flattering words from those who would exploit our country and her resources. Join us in working toward peace. Fight for freedom. For Libya!"

They all heard the cheers from the soldiers near the gate. Atwah's fists were clenched tightly, and his face was red from rage. "Death to the enemies of Libya!" he shouted. He took a wild shot toward the gate, then turned his gun back on Rian.

This was it. With one last look around her, Rian raised her face to the sky. The sun was starting to set and one lone star blinked in the deep blue of a day that was about to end.

Just like her life.

Maybe she would soon be looking down at the earth like that star.

She heard the gunshot and at the same moment felt herself shoved to the ground. She landed awkwardly with someone on top of her. Pushing on the weight, she saw Omar's face above her.

"I'm sorry," he gasped, his breaths rattling through him. "But you must run. Go to safety."

No sooner had he spoken than gunfire broke out all around her. A small explosion went off just to her right. Smoke began to fill the air.

"Rian!"

She wriggled out from under Omar, whose sightless eyes attested to his death, when she saw Augie crawling toward her. He grabbed her hand. "We've got to get out of here. Come on!"

They kept their heads low and started running toward the gate. Bullets kicked up the dust at their feet and near their head. It felt as if they were right in the crossfire of two much larger armies. Which they were.

Moving behind an abandoned pickup truck, Augie leaned against the back tire, his breath coming in gasps. "We've got to get to that gate."

She looked at the distance between them and the gate. Explosions and machine-gun fire sounded all around them without any pauses. "We've cheated death once already today. Do we dare press our luck a second time?"

His lips lifted in an adorable and confident grin. "Well, I am wearing my lucky shirt. Sure, it's a little torn in the back, but it still has its magic."

Pulled into his daring mood, she took a deep breath and reached for his hand. "Okay then. Let's go."

CHAPTER ELEVEN

Augie had never run faster in his entire life. Dust and smoke obscured his vision, but the sound of bullets so close to his head kept him sprinting toward the gate, Rian's hand clasped firmly in his. He wasn't going to lose her now.

The bullets coming from behind them seemed to pause, and Augie quickly glanced up. Malek and several other soldiers were laying down cover fire for them. Putting on an extra burst of speed, Augie and Rian ran through the defensive line near the gate. They dashed behind a concrete wall and quickly got down. Several soldiers were holding their positions there, guns at the ready. Malek squatted beside Augie and Rian.

"Where's Colt?" Augie asked, his breaths coming in gasps.

"Your friends are waiting for you in the command center. The General decided it was best for them to hang back for now." Malek didn't even flinch when the soldiers at the other end of the wall started shooting again. "I'll take you to them."

Augie fought to catch his breath and turned to Rian. "See? My lucky shirt came through for us."

She tried to laugh, but gasped instead, her hands on her knees. "Yes. Your lucky shirt and Malek's good aim."

"That, too." He grinned. Making sure her hand was firmly in his, they followed Malek and an armed guard to the command center. The image of Fahad's gun to her temple was still fresh in Augie's mind, and he wanted to keep her close for as long as he could.

Malek led them to a one-story office building that looked like it had taken hard mortar fire at one point. They picked their way through a long and darkened hallway and ended up in a large room that was mostly intact with a dozen monitors in the corner. Colt turned and strode across the room to meet them.

"Augie, I can't tell you how good it is to see you standing in front of me. I was worried for a minute there when I realized you were with Atwah." Colt put his hand on Augie's shoulder. "We've got a lot to discuss."

"I'm just glad you're all here. I wasn't entirely sure my message got through." Augie had to let go of Rian's hand as Colt steered him toward the monitors. Augie twisted his head around to see where she was going.

Colt didn't seem to notice Augie's inattention and kept talking as they walked. "The oil terminal has an extensive security system, so even though Atwah always has multiple exit strategies, we can use that to keep eyes on him. If we lose him now, there's no telling when we'll have another chance to get him back in custody."

Augie finally gave up on trying to see where Rian and Malek were headed and faced the rest of the team near the security monitors. The person in the middle of them all stood as soon as he came near.

"Don't ever scare me like that again." Brenna hugged him and motioned toward the chair she'd just vacated. "The cameras cover a lot of the terminal, but I haven't been able to spot Atwah since the fighting broke out. I could use some help."

Augie sat down quickly and took stock of what was in front of him. Considering they were in a building that didn't even have a front door, it was surprising to see a sophisticated security system hidden in the middle of it. He looked at each of the monitors in front of him. "Do we know where the Prime Minister is? The last couple of days, Atwah has seemed particularly focused on him and the ceremonial hand-off of Ras Lanuf."

"As soon as we got your location and figured out you were likely in Atwah's custody, the meeting was called off." Colt leaned in, his palm spread on the table as he stared at the monitors in front of them. "We tried to have General Saleh hang back as well, but he insisted on being in the fight with his men."

It felt natural to be back in the thick of things with the team around him, but strange, too. He'd been with Rian 24/7 for the last several days, and he was already missing having her close. He glanced to his left. Where was she?

It didn't take him long to find her. She was a few feet away in the corner of the room, standing in front of Malek. He was staring at her as if he'd never seen her before. In a way, he hadn't. Augie leaned over his table, trying to hear what they were saying without being obvious.

"How did I not guess you are a woman?" Malek asked, his voice carrying over the noise of the room.

She lifted her shoulder in a half-shrug, a little crease of worry in her forehead, but still standing tall in front of her friend. "I'm sorry. I hope you can understand why I did it."

Augie wished he were by her side, facing the questions with her. Of course, she didn't need him, but he still wanted her to feel his support. Seeing her as a woman had to be a shock to Malek, especially since they'd worked together for so long.

Colt's voice interrupted and pulled him back to the monitors. "He's got to be here somewhere." Everyone was totally focused on finding Atwah. Augie needed to get his head in the game so he could do his part.

Augie sat on the edge of his chair. Stretching his fingers, he got down to business, starting with figuring out the video management software to see what features this security system had and what the recording settings were. Augie wanted to make sure he had a handle on exactly what was in front of him. If this security system was the key to finding Atwah, he was going to make sure it was running at peak performance. After everything Atwah had put him and Rian through, he wanted the man in custody as soon as possible, now more than ever.

Brenna, Nate, Elliot, and Abby all surrounded the monitors now, each of them riveted to the screens.

"We've got a fire near the front gate." Brenna pointed to a monitor. "Looks like several tire fires in a pattern." Black smoke was already starting to obscure any visuals, and Augie groaned inwardly. That was going to make surveillance a lot harder. "Hey, it looks like some of the soldiers Atwah came with have joined General Saleh," she added.

It was true. A group of soldiers had joined with the ones standing guard on the perimeter. "Small victories like that could turn the battle into the General's favor," Augie said, seeing some movement in the upper right corner monitor. "When did you and Elliot get to Libya?" he asked Brenna, while he did his best to enhance the image on the screen.

"As soon as Colt got your location and realized you might be traveling with Atwah, he smuggled us all in. Mya found a contact in the U.N. that was familiar with the situation in Libya, so she's working that angle with Jake." She squinted at the image Augie was enhancing. "What's going on up there? And where is that in the complex, exactly?"

The black smoke from the tire fires combined with the smoke bombs and the sunset, made visibility extremely low. They could still see soldiers from both groups running in several directions, trying to find cover wherever they could.

"I'm not sure what that building is," he said. He bit his thumbnail, watching dozens of men converging on what looked like a medium-sized warehouse. "It's on the opposite end of the terminal, near the polyethylene processing plant," he pointed out. That couldn't be good.

A familiar figure approached the warehouse at the bottom of the screen. Atwah. Fahad was at his side, and they strode into the warehouse with barely a nod for the soldiers who were lining up outside.

"Atwah is there." Augie pointed "With at least a dozen soldiers."

"We better head over there. He's got to be setting something up from that warehouse, and it's too close to a lot of flammable chemicals." Colt turned to the team. "Grab the rest of your gear, and we'll head over there."

Augie kept his eyes on the monitors to make sure Atwah didn't leave. He moved closer when he spotted three black town cars approaching the warehouse. He blinked twice, hoping he wasn't really seeing the cars onscreen. One of them sported flags waving on either side of the car. That could only mean one thing.

"Prime Minister al-Masli is definitely not coming here today, is he Colt?" His blood ran cold at the implications of what was happening right before his eyes.

"Right. We left him safe at the hotel." Colt turned to him as he redid the Velcro on his tactical vest. "Why?"

Augie pointed at the screen. "Look at that convoy approaching.

I think al-Masli is here at Ras Lanuf and just pulled up to the warehouse that Atwah is in."

Colt's jaw clenched as he watched the images on the screen. "What does he think he's doing? We've got to get over there. Now."

Augie felt sick. "Colt, Atwah had me hack General Saleh's emails. He could have sent instructions to the Prime Minister that would have looked like they came from the General. Maybe that's why he didn't stay at the hotel."

"We'll have to sort that out later. Let's concentrate on what we do know." Colt turned just as Malek and Rian joined the group, both of them dressed in the same tactical gear that Griffin Force had.

"What's going on?" Malek asked Abby who was standing closest to him.

"The Prime Minister is here and Atwah is about to ambush him." She looked down at her tactical gear. "Good thing we came ready for the fight."

Colt wound a keffiyeh around his head, and the rest of the team did the same. That would help them all blend in a little better, especially the women in the group. He quickly handed a comm set to Augie and earpieces for both Malek and Rian. "We've got to get over there. Stay on comms and don't take your eyes off Atwah." He turned to Rian and Malek. "I'm assuming you're with us?"

Malek looked down at Rian, his eyebrows raised. "I'm going, but whether you come or not is up to you."

"Let's go, then." Rian turned to leave, but gave Augie a little wave and a smile before she disappeared down the hallway.

Be safe, he thought. For just a second, Augie wanted to grab a gun and head out beside her and his team, but that had never been part of this job for him. He would be more helpful in his usual role at the command center.

Turning back to the screen he watched the convoy stop in front of the warehouse Atwah had entered moments earlier. Prime Minister al-Masli got out with two other men and several bodyguards. The door of the warehouse opened, and Atwah appeared, his arms outstretched. He was speaking, but the security footage didn't have audio. Augie could only guess at what he was saying.

Augie leaned closer, wanting to reach out and stop what was happening. "No, no, no," he murmured. If the Prime Minister were killed, the country would descend further into chaos and the peace process would be set back indefinitely. But Atwah would know that and would do everything he could to take advantage of the situation.

The Prime Minister obviously recognized who was in front of him and immediately retreated back toward his car. One of his bodyguards did his best to shield al-Masli and hustle him into the vehicle to safety. He wrenched the door open and the Prime Minister dove into the backseat. His bodyguard followed, still using his body to shield his boss from any danger.

And then gunfire broke out.

The car was riddled with bullets from the AK-47s, but they weren't penetrating. Augie smiled a little at that. Armored cars. Smart. But that triumph was short-lived. There was a flash of movement from the side of the screen as one of Atwah's men threw a grenade. Thankfully, it rolled too far and landed underneath the car behind the one the Prime Minister was currently in. Within seconds it exploded, twisting the car on its side, but leaving the Prime Minister's intact. Augie leaned his head against his hand and massaged his temples. That had been too close, and only showed that these men didn't care if they killed the Prime Minister. He'd thought Atwah would at least try to bargain for the Prime Minister's life.

"Augie, give me a sit rep," Colt said, his voice crackling over their comms.

"The Prime Minister made it back inside the car with one of his bodyguards. Atwah's men threw a grenade, but it overshot and blew up the car behind al-Masli's." He looked closer at the screen. "The two other men and the rest of the bodyguards are surrounded by Atwah's men in front of the warehouse. How close are you?"

"Five minutes out," Colt told him, his breaths staggered as if he was running.

Five minutes out was too long. The Prime Minister needed help now. "I still can't see you." Augie scanned the monitors close to the warehouse, then checked all of them to stay on top of what was happening on the rest of the security feeds. The pockets of fighting seemed to be intensifying throughout the complex, but it was impossible to tell who had the upper hand.

He came back to the screen that showed the warehouse where Atwah was, and the images in front of him stalled the words in his mouth. He forced them out. "Atwah dragged one of the Prime Minister's men to the window of the car. He's got a gun to the back of his head."

Augie sat back in his chair. The Prime Minister would have a front row seat to the man's murder if he did nothing. Would he open the car door to save the man? Augie hoped not for the Prime Minister's sake, but also couldn't imagine watching someone you knew die for you. "Colt, the Prime Minister just opened the car door. We're too late."

The team finally came into the camera's view and they *were* close. Could they get there in time? Augie leaned in. "Come on," he said out loud, unable to take his eyes off the screen. "Colt, you're close. We can still do this."

But Atwah was marching the Prime Minister inside the warehouse. And in that moment, everything became clear all at once.

This had been Atwah's plan all along. He wasn't here just to take over the oil terminal and use the money to finance his terrorist organization. He was here to take the oil terminal for the money *and* kidnap the Prime Minister for the power, then kill him when he was of no more use. This was a coup. He wanted to make Libya his own little kingdom if he could.

And they might not be able to stop either one of them from happening.

Augie took a deep breath as he watched the team crest the last ridge before they reached the warehouse. The Prime Minister was still outside. "Hurry," he said, adrenaline coursing through him. "We can't let it end like this."

With so many lives on the line and the freedom of a country at stake, everything depended on what happened next.

CHAPTER TWELVE

R ian ran alongside Malek, keeping her eyes trained on
the way ahead. They crested a small hill and saw the
still-burning car in front of the warehouse. The Prime
Minister's car's passenger door was open, but no one was paying
any attention to it. They were following Atwah and the Prime
Minister into the building.

Colt held up his hand, and the team stopped behind him.
"Okay, the Prime Minister is inside so that changes our mission."

They retreated back behind the small hill they'd just come
from. Colt squatted down next to Malek. "What do we know about
that warehouse?"

"It's used for equipment storage. There are two floors." Malek
wiped the sweat from his brow. "There's a way in from the back of
the building, but I'm sure Atwah will have guards on the
perimeter."

"We need a distraction," Nate said, looking over at the warehouse. "Something that could draw them out, or at least some of
the guards."

"Any suggestions?" Colt asked, looking at the team.

Rian glanced around their position. "What about blowing something up? Not something that would start a chain explosion, of course, but enough to draw their attention."

Augie's voice came over the comms. "What if we drive one of the buses from the training camp over where you guys are? Make sure it's far enough away not to do any damage to the refinery or anything else and then blow it?"

"I don't know if we have time for that," Abby said, looking over at Malek. "What about some of these pickup trucks and vehicles that are all over this place? They look pretty much abandoned. Do we have enough explosives to blow two or three close to the warehouse?"

"Definitely. And I think I should update General Saleh about what's going on with the Prime Minister." Malek looked over at the warehouse. "I suspect we'll need his help to finish this."

"Augie, how's the fighting looking at the front gate?" Colt asked.

"The tires are still burning, but it looks like most of the fighting is moving toward the south side." He sounded calm, as if reporting on the weather and not the fight they were in.

Rian pressed the earpiece further into her ear. It was strange to have Augie's voice in her head, but comforting at the same time. It surprised her a little bit how attached she'd become to him.

"Malek, you take Elliot and start setting the explosives. We'll get into position, then give you the signal. Be quick and careful. We can't afford to lose either of you." Colt looked at the rest of them. "We'll get as close to the warehouse as we can so that as soon as the explosion triggers and the guards leave their post, we can move in."

Elliot nodded and half-stood. "You be c-careful, too, boss."

Colt acknowledged his words, and the two men started making

The spotlight was trained on the Prime Minister and two other men. They sat in chairs, lined up in a row, their hands zip tied in front of them. Soldiers holding AK-47s stood behind each chair, the guns pointed at the back of their skulls.

And Atwah was standing behind a large camera trained on the men. "Now you will tell the world why I should be the ruler of Libya," he announced, walking around the camera and coming to stand right in front of Prime Minister al-Masli. "You will give me your blessing to do the job you should have been man enough to do. And if you don't, the world will watch your execution."

CHAPTER THIRTEEN

ugie had never listened to his comms more closely than he was now. He could see from the security monitors that the guards were still poking around outside the warehouse, but he hadn't heard any chatter from the Griffin Force members who were inside. The wait to get an update was excruciating. Even reciting his favorite binomials or theorems wouldn't work to calm him this time.

Colt's voice finally sounded in his ear. "Atwah has a camera set up in here, Augie. Can you trace a signal on it?"

Augie pulled the laptop closer and did his best to look for any signals coming from the warehouse location, but couldn't find an obvious one. "I'm not seeing anything from my end, but it's possible he could still hook into Libya's State TV, since the government was planning to televise the handoff ceremony. Maybe Atwah hijacked one of the news vans."

Nate's voice chimed in. "Do you have any idea who the other two men are with the Prime Minister?"

"Negative. The ceremony was supposed to include some U.N. representatives, though. It could be them." Augie wished he had eyes inside the warehouse so he could be of more help. "Can you take out the soldiers? Or does anyone have a clear shot at Atwah?"

Colt answered immediately. "Negative. Prime Minister al-Masli has an AK-47 pointed at him and what looks like an explosive vest on."

Augie's ribcage squeezed at Colt's words. If Atwah had rigged explosives to the Prime Minister, then there was a good chance no one was getting out of there alive. Once Atwah had what he wanted, he was going to blow up the warehouse, or at least the people in it, no matter what anyone did.

"Do we have a plan?" Augie tapped his fingers on the table. There had to be something they could do. But what?

Nate grunted. "Well, we can't shoot Atwah. It looks like he has a trigger for the vest in his hand." He let out an audible breath.

Augie looked at the screen. "What if we find the control room and cut the power? Then Atwah wouldn't be able to broadcast. Then we could pull out our night-vision goggles to get the hostages to safety." It would take a lot of precision, though, with that many guns and no lights.

"That might work." Colt was quiet for a moment. "Is there any cover at all if we can get downstairs?"

Augie looked at the building schematics. "Possibly. The far corner has two smaller storage rooms that are accessible if you go down the elevator shaft."

Colt was quick to respond. "Copy that. We'll meet at the elevator shaft and get ready for a lights-out scenario."

Augie was keeping an eye on the outside of the warehouse when he saw a large burst of light. The rumble from an explosion came through his comms at the same time. Were Malek and Elliot still blowing up cars? Or was this something else? "What's going on over there?" he asked.

But no one answered.

The laptop chirped that he had an alert. Augie pressed his earpiece closer to his ear so he could hear even the tiniest whisper from the team. Opening up the alert, he could see that Libyan State TV had come online. The Prime Minister was on camera, looking grim. The explosion had been a powerful enough blast that it knocked over equipment and barrels behind them, but no one seemed seriously hurt.

"Radio check," Augie said again into the comms.

Brenna, Abby, and Colt all checked in, but Nate and Rian didn't. Augie gripped the edge of the table. Something was wrong.

Yelling was coming through the comms, but Augie couldn't make out what they were saying or who exactly was speaking. Then Nate's voice came through. "We're compromised. Stay on mission."

Those five words hit Augie like a stack of textbooks falling directly on him. Nate and Rian were captured and Atwah wanted them both dead. Dread curled in his gut. He wished he could see exactly what was going on, but all he could do was listen.

He got his wish moments later when Nate and Rian were dragged in front of the camera, stripped of tactical gear, and forced to kneel in front of Atwah. He stared down at them, his arms folded, as if he were the devil himself delivering judgment on the mere mortals in front of him.

Pivoting to face the camera, Atwah pointed to Nate and Rian. "Libya has enemies in her midst. Even in our most-guarded regions. Foreigners. One of our own citizens." He pointed to the Prime Minister. "And now we find that Libya's leaders have betrayed her as well. Libya needs real leaders, not cowards who reach out to foreign powers to make a sham peace while they plunder Libya's resources." He stared into the camera and his black eyes were like magnets, drawing people to his words, to his natural charisma.

No wonder he's been able to convert so many to his cause, Augie thought.

"My men are even now fighting for Libya. We have crushed the so-called peace accord that your Prime Minister was attempting to bind you to, and we will keep fighting to put power back in the hands of those who can bear the weight of it." He turned to the Prime Minister with a flourish. "You have failed, but if you join us now, and encourage your people to fall in line with my cause, you may still have a place in Libya."

Prime Minister al-Masli slowly stood, his eyes on Atwah. His hands were still zip tied, his clothes disheveled, but his proud bearing was not diminished. "The people of Libya have lost and sacrificed too much trying to get rid of one dictator just to replace him with another. You speak of foreigners who would plunder our land. You speak of yourself! I know who you are, Mahmoud Atwah. You are nothing but a thief and a murderer and no true Libyan would ever support you." He spit on the ground near Atwah's feet. "Libyans will always fight for freedom."

Atwah strode forward and backhanded the Prime Minister and he went down hard. "Coward!" Atwah said, standing over him. He turned to face the camera once again. "The people of Libya will choose between a peace that would have you under a boot of obligation to other countries for decades, or taking their place of prestige on the world stage with power and money. *That* is what Libya deserves. We can show this country's glory and power without bowing to anyone. But first we must rid ourselves of our enemies."

Augie's heart skipped a beat. Was Atwah going to kill all his prisoners on live TV? Rian and Nate were still kneeling on the floor, just barely visible on the corner of the screen. Fahad toed Nate with his boot, but Nate barely lifted his head, as if he was saying a fervent prayer that couldn't be interrupted.

A prayer might not be a bad idea, Augie thought. *Certainly couldn't hurt.*

But Atwah was still playing to the camera and moved to stand in front of Nate, waving dramatically toward his kneeling form. "I have met this traitor before. His ties to the American CIA are well-known. The same agency who plays both sides of any war, and then claim no knowledge. The same country who betrays everyone they've ever signed a treaty with, but say they are only fighting for the greater good." He gave a mirthless laugh. "Americans aren't fit to lick our boots."

Atwah leaned down close to Nate's ear, out of sound range from the camera, but Nate's earpiece still picked up his words. "Abby betrayed me and I promised I would have my revenge. Since I can't finish my business with her, I'd like to send her a message. Be sure to pass it along." He motioned to Fahad. The guard brought his gun up and slammed the stock down on the back of Nate's head. He crumpled to the ground, unconscious.

"No, no, no," Augie murmured softly.

Abby's muffled cry into the comms tore out his heart. But it wasn't over yet. Atwah was going to go down the line of prisoners, Augie knew it. That was Atwah's M.O. to maim, hurt, or kill anyone he deemed an enemy. Rian was next.

Fahad stepped over Nate's prone form on the floor and nudged Rian forward. Atwah grabbed her arm and hauled her to her feet.

"This woman," he sneered, "has dressed as a boy for many years to disguise herself as a messenger to the revolution leaders in

Benghazi. Because of this deception, she has had access to the highest levels of government and now we find her in the company of someone who works with the CIA?" Atwah tutted. "Those who betray us must pay the ultimate price."

Augie put his hand over his mouth, his stomach churning with nausea. This could not be happening. Atwah was going to kill her, and all he could do was watch.

Fahad moved behind her, but he didn't have his gun. He had another explosive vest. The moment Rian realized what was about to happen, she fought it, her fist connecting with Fahad's jaw at least twice, but two more guards were called over to hold her down while the vest was placed on her.

Augie couldn't sit still anymore. He stood and started pacing, unable to take his eyes from the screen. Rian's face was flushed, but she stood there with her fists clenched, giving Atwah a murderous glare.

"You can kill me," she said, her voice clear and unafraid, "but you'll never kill all of us who fight against people like you."

Atwah held up the trigger---a small cell phone. "Hold your tongue, or you will lose it. The vest will take care of your lying mouth."

Colt's voice cut into Augie's thoughts. "Can you zero in on the signal coming from that vest? Maybe we can jam it and move in."

Flustered that he hadn't even thought of the rest of the team for several minutes, Augie sat down. *Focus*, he told himself. *Do your job.*

Augie searched for anything that could help them, but came up empty. "If there's a signal, it's not strong enough to hack. Are you and the team safe?"

"For now. But we've got to get Nate and Rian out of there, and our options are limited." Colt's voice was normally gruff, but when he said their names it had an extra edge. He was worried.

Before Augie could say anything else, the State TV feed that had been showing Rian's face as she was told to sit on the floor suddenly went black.

Augie quickly tried to refresh, needing to see her onscreen, but nothing helped. Comms were still open, though, and Augie leaned his head in his hands to listen. Was she okay? He needed to hear for himself.

"Rian, if you can hear me, clear your throat." She did and the sound was like music to Augie's ears. "I need to know more about your vest so we can disarm it and you get you out of there. Are there any wires coming out of it?"

"Two," she whispered. "Red and green."

Atwah was speaking in the background about unfinished business and going to Tripoli. His voice was muffled, so he must have turned his back to her.

"Can you see a detonator anywhere on the vest?" Augie asked.

"No. But maybe the cell phone has a code to detonate mine and a different one for the Prime Minister?" Her voice sounded strained but calm.

"That's good intel. I'll look into that." He gripped the table in front of him. "Do you have anything around you that could possibly be used to cut a wire?"

"Yes, I have a knife in my sleeve," she whispered. "But---"

Whatever she was about to say was cut off with Atwah's voice. "Somehow these two infiltrated our operation, and I don't think they were alone. I want every inch of this building searched and any other spies brought to me. Once they are taken care of, we can go triumphant to Tripoli to claim the spoils of our victory."

Augie's blood ran cold. They were going to search the warehouse? With limited places to hide that meant . . . "Colt," he started.

Colt's voice overrode his. "Everyone take cover."

Biting his nail, Augie listened for any other communication. None came. Everyone in the field was good at what they did, even

Rian. She'd shown that the entire time they'd been with Atwah. But he just had to say it. "Rian, I'm going to get you out of this."

Her voice was soft, but he heard her loud and clear. "I know."

Her vote of confidence sparked the optimism he usually had while he was on an operation. He bent over his laptop. He was going to do everything he could to keep his promise.

CHAPTER FOURTEEN

The heaviness of the vest wrapped around her body matched the heaviness Rian felt. She'd cheated death several times in the last twenty-four hours, but her time might really be up now. She didn't see how they could escape this one unscathed. Though everything looked bleak at the moment, she was glad to have her earpiece still. It was small enough that no one had noticed it. Knowing the team was out there trying to help her was the only hope she had.

Looking down at Nate unconscious on the floor, her heart squeezed. Blood pooled underneath his head. He needed medical attention, and fast, but Atwah would never allow that. She'd been surprised to hear Atwah mention Abby. How did he know both Nate and Abby? What had their dealings been in the past?

One of the men who had come in with the Prime Minister leaned forward and looked down at her on the floor. "Are you okay?"

She looked up at him and knit her brows together. He had a high forehead, dark brown hair, and a stubborn jawline. His face looked vaguely familiar, but he was a westerner. Perhaps the General had met with him before when she'd been present? Or Malek?

"I'm fine," she managed to get out. She looked away, but could feel his eyes on her still. Bending her knees, she stared straight ahead. Hopefully the man wouldn't call any attention to them and try to speak to her again.

Atwah's soldiers were still searching the building for Griffin Force, and while Rian hoped they didn't find anyone, the search took the scrutiny off the hostages for the moment. Atwah's attention was elsewhere, so she took advantage of the small reprieve. Rolling her neck, she tried to relax as much as she could while wearing a suicide vest that could end her life at any moment.

Glancing up, she caught the man still staring at her, his dark brown eyes looking down at her with shock and . . . caring. And that's when she knew. He wasn't familiar because he'd been in a meeting with Libyan leaders. She'd seen that look of caring on his face before. Frowning, she tried to look away, but he spoke to her again.

"What's your name?" he whispered.

She didn't want to talk to him or look at him. She wanted to forget she'd seen him. Speaking to him only brought back memories she'd spent years burying deep inside. But a small part of her was curious. Would he give her the answers she needed? Where had he been all these years?

Licking her lips, she folded her hands in her lap. "Rian."

"Ask him what his job is, why he's here," Augie said into her ear.

Rian jolted a bit at Augie's voice. She'd forgotten he could hear everything going on through her earpiece.

"What's your job? Why are you here?" she repeated, feeling a bit robotic. She needed to get a handle on her emotions.

"My name is Steven Perron. I'm the U.N. Special Envoy to Libya." He said his words slowly and watched for her reaction.

Rian kept her face blank. This had to be a coincidence. One of Atwah's tricks. There was no way her father would be here. He'd left them and never looked back. This man couldn't be him. But Atwah couldn't have known about their connection, could he? She didn't know what to think.

"I'll get a full background on Perron right away," Augie said in her ear. "Good work, Rian."

His words registered in her mind, but the echo of her father's name still reverberated through her whole being. Steven Perron. Steven Ryan Perron, who was once sent to the U.S. consulate in Benghazi. Who abandoned his wife and daughter. Her gaze cut to him again, seeing the tiny scar he'd always had at the edge of his right eyebrow. He'd told her when she was a girl that he'd gotten the scar trying to learn to skateboard. She pursed her lips, hurt and anger washing over her. Did he regret leaving them? Why was he really here?

His eyes met hers, tears welling in them as he looked at her. Rian glanced away. To see him again was so overwhelming, she didn't know what to do with the knife-like pain slicing through her heart. What could she even say to him?

"Rian," her father said. He wanted her to look at him. She raised her face to do so, but Malek's voice came over her earpiece.

"If anyone on the team can hear me, I want to give you a heads up. General Saleh is on his way to the warehouse. He wants to meet with Atwah face to face." Malek's voice sounded uncertain, something Rian rarely heard from him. He always seemed so sure of himself and what the next step should be. But even she knew the General walking into this warehouse was a bad idea. That would be giving Atwah exactly what he wanted.

Colt was obviously thinking along the same lines. "Stop him,

Malek. If he comes here, Atwah will have all the advantages. He could kill both the General and the Prime Minister, which would plunge Libya into an even deeper crisis." Colt's voice was low and urgent. "Tell him no."

"I can't. When the General was apprised of the situation, he was adamant that he stand up to Atwah and show the country the difference between them." Malek was apologetic now. "We are almost to you now, accompanied by a dozen men."

Rian could barely keep the surprise off her face. What was the General thinking? This could end very badly. For all of them.

Two of Atwah's men came into the room and whispered to Fahad. From the look on Fahad's face, he was not expecting the message he'd just gotten. He moved to Atwah's side. "The General is outside requesting a meeting with you, *padrone*."

Atwah looked pleased. "Show him in." As soon as the guards had left to do his bidding, he moved to the corner with Fahad, where the two men conferred, whispering together and occasionally looking at the Prime Minister. If only she were closer and could hear what they were planning!

The General swept in with Malek and another man at his side. He didn't waste any time and walked straight up to Atwah. "Stop this madness right now. Call your men back before all of them are killed and their sacrifice at your command counted for nothing." He swept an arm toward the Prime Minister. "We can continue our peace accord and forget any of this ever happened."

Atwah listened patiently while the General spoke, as if he were a parent listening to the ramblings of a child. When the General stopped talking, Atwah stroked his beard. "You do not give the orders here." He walked to the side of the general, forcing him to turn if he wanted to keep Atwah in his sight. "I find it quite naïve of you to suppose that my men are not committed to do everything they can to take over this oil terminal. But they are eager to once again be part of a government that is propelling Libya to be a world power."

"I've already been told of your empty promises to them. They're only committed because of your assurances that they would have money and power---two things you do not have in your possession and cannot possibly deliver." The General gave Atwah a derisive once-over.

Atwah's jaw tightened in annoyance. "You have asked for a meeting, General, and you shall have it. Please, sit down." Fahad brought a chair and set it next to Prime Minister al-Masli. "Shall we turn the camera on so all of Libya can hear what you have to say?"

General Saleh dipped his head. "Of course. I'm not afraid to speak to my people."

"Excellent. It occurs to me that with the Prime Minister in attendance, as well as yourself, along with some of your esteemed colleagues from the U.N., we could hold a tribunal, if you will. Let each of us state our vision for Libya, and the people can witness a new leader for Libya being chosen. On live TV." Atwah gave him a satisfied smile, looking between the Prime Minister and the General for their reaction.

Rian's mouth dropped open in surprise. A tribunal to choose the country's leader. Even if such a council were legal, Atwah would never accept the results if they weren't in his favor. And Libya's freedom would not come this way. They needed democratic elections, not a sham tribunal with a terrorist holding them all hostage.

"Once the case is made, and you are not chosen, you will leave Libya. Immediately." The General made a commanding figure, though his uniform was dusty and rumpled. He'd been out with his men today, in the thick of the fighting. That said something about his character.

Atwah merely lifted the corners of his mouth in a tight-lipped smile. "We'll see who is the victor. Once we've all spoken for ourselves, the winner will be clear and the people will fall in line." Atwah seemed very self-assured. Something else was going on here, but Rian didn't know what. She looked around at Atwah's men. They were all staring at him like he was a revered leader. Or had he blinded them with his empty promises, as well? Did everyone believe his lies of riches and power if they supported him?

"Augie? Can you hear what's being said?" she whispered, hoping he was still there. He hadn't said anything for a while.

"I can hear it." Augie sounded grim. "What is the General thinking?"

"He's doing what he does best, fighting for his country. He's also stalling and giving us time to get into position." Colt sounded so close when he spoke. The earpiece picked his voice up so well, it was like he was right next to her.

"Let's put a plan together. We don't have much time." Abby's voice had a thread of worry in it that she couldn't hide. Of course, with Nate still unconscious, she would be anxious to get to him.

"I'm working on the angles," Augie said. "Just give me a few more minutes."

Rian's gaze moved over the room. Atwah was standing near the camera while Fahad got everything set up. Nate was still next to her on the floor. His breathing was even and steady, so that helped her not worry so much. She reached up, unwound the keffiyeh from her shoulders, and put it under his head, hoping to slow the bleeding. He stirred a little when she touched him. That was a good sign.

"Abby, Nate's going to be okay," she said, keeping her voice barely above a whisper. "He's coming around a bit."

"Thanks, Rian," Abby said softly.

Once she was sure Nate was settled as much as he could be, Rian looked at the rest of the men in the room, and Steven Perron came into view. He didn't flinch, his eyes staring back at hers. Their shape was familiar---her own eyes were tilted exactly the same way. But she didn't want it to be true.

How could she be meeting her father again after all these years, when her life was in the hands of a madman? It was a cruel twist of fate.

But fate had been kind to her so far. Maybe there would be one more chance to find out what had happened and why he'd never come back for them.

All they had to do was make it out of this alive.

CHAPTER FIFTEEN

Augie hated to be grateful to Atwah for anything, but he would have told the man thank you ten times over when the cameras turned back on and Augie could see what was going on inside that warehouse instead of just hearing bits and pieces.

Atwah was posing in front of the camera again, dramatically pointing to the man who'd said his name was Steven Perron. "This man is the U.N. Special Envoy to Libya. He tells us he wants unity for Libya and has been working for that for many years. Today, we will see just how true his statements are. It is providence that General Saleh and Prime Minister al-Masli, are here with me now, and we will hold a tribunal. Mr. Perron will tell us who can unify Libya and is fit to be her leader."

Mr. Perron grimaced before he held up his zip tied hands and motioned toward the explosive vest strapped to the Prime Minister. "Mr. Atwah, since we are being held hostage and these proceedings are under duress, nothing decided here would be binding."

"The people's will would be binding. They will see the choices before them and know who is destined to lead." Atwah looked at the camera, his hands on his hips. He switched to Arabic and addressed the viewers. "It is my destiny that has brought me to this point. I have spent my life building a coalition of followers from all around the world, people who believe that I was chosen to show the way to those who are lost. I am the one who can smooth the path for Libya to reclaim her former glory. I've proved my leadership by successfully fighting westerners and any who oppose me. They fear me."

Steven spoke up. "Mr. Atwah, can you speak about the fact that you are wanted for war crimes in several countries?"

"*Oufft*, who has made such accusations? The so-called 'allied' forces that we ran out of Afghanistan and Iraq? People who are my enemies? No one of importance I can assure you." Atwah flicked his hand as if flicking the words from the air. "I have committed no crimes, only fought in wars that others started."

Augie shook his head at that statement. He'd read mountains of paperwork on all the people Atwah had killed himself or had ordered killed. He'd once had his own secret police force who were the most-feared group in all of Iraq. Atwah had many crimes to answer for, whether he acknowledged them or not.

General Saleh stood, as if impatient with the show Atwah was obviously putting on. He straightened his coat and faced the camera. "My people know me and what I've done for them. My own blood was spilled for Libya during the fight for freedom. My heart has always been in this land." He thumped his fist over the left side of his chest for emphasis.

"Come, come, General, let's be truthful," Atwah interrupted. "You cut off oil production to starve the people and bend them to your will. You conspired with foreign nations for arms to fight your countrymen. You fought with Gaddafi and accepted protection from the Americans, did you not?" When the General didn't answer, he pressed his point. "Do you deny it?"

General Saleh gave him a steely-eyed glare. "I was educated in war and diplomacy and was taught the value of being a Libyan and all that means. Can you say the same?"

"I, too, was educated in war and diplomacy, but I will never lick another country's boot. I will come from a place of strength and force *them* to bend." Atwah raised his eyebrows. "That is what a real leader does."

"This peace accord would have been a place of strength and a boon to our people. Now you are stirring old wounds and trying to overthrow all that we have worked for." The General's voice was getting louder. Any thread of patience he was trying to hold onto was at the breaking point. "I know what you did in Iraq, Syria, and Afghanistan. I know of your ties to Iran. Your heart is black and selfish, and you only have *your* interests in mind."

Atwah moved in front of the general, his mouth twisted in a scornful look. "I, too, know of what you did to help bring Gaddafi to power and the atrocities you committed while you served in his army." He pointed his finger in General Saleh's face. "You are not quite as pure as you want others to think."

The General leaned in so close that Atwah's finger nearly touched his cheek. "And I was also the one who was on the frontline to topple Gaddafi's reign of terror over this country. It was I who recognized the need for a free and peaceful Libya and have given my life to achieve that." His voice was like a drill sergeant informing a new recruit of his duties. It was easy to see why he was a formidable commander.

Augie's Arabic was good enough to catch most of what had been said. He tried to get a read on the room from the limited view of the camera. From what he could tell, everyone was riveted to the drama in front of them. It wasn't every day that you had a known terrorist confronting a country's leaders in a forced tribunal. If Libya's State TV had ratings, this would probably top any broadcast they'd ever had before.

Atwah put his hand down, but stayed toe-to-toe with the General. He waved his fingers behind him in the direction of the Prime Minister. "You say you have been working for peace, yet you have been fighting this man and his forces for years. Can you honestly say you don't want him dead?"

The General was quiet for a moment, and Augie wondered if Atwah had finally hit a nerve. Saleh shifted for a moment before he directed his gaze to the Prime Minister. "It's true, I have wanted him dead. But now I see that peace with him and working together with his government is what will benefit the country most. And that's what today was supposed to be about. The first steps toward peace."

Augie's eyes watched the screen. Atwah had turned at those words, obviously not getting the answer he wanted from General Saleh. He began pacing back and forth and with each turn, came closer to where Rian was sitting. Since he couldn't jam any signals coming from the phone or the vest, they had to get that phone.

"Rian, can you see the phone in Atwah's hand?" Augie asked over comms.

"Yes," she murmured.

"If we turn off the lights when he's closest to you, do you think you could grab it?" Augie had to suck in a breath after he said it. The idea was so dangerous. The timing would have to be perfect. If it wasn't, both vests could go off and kill everyone in the room.

"I think I can do it," she said without hesitation. "But give me some warning on when it's going to happen."

"I will." Augie double-checked the building schematics. They still needed someone in the control room to pull the control bar on the central circuit breaker. As he searched for the best way to get there from the elevator shaft, Jake's face popped up on his screen. Augie pressed the video call accept button and muted his comms. "Hey, Jake, tell me you have some good news for us."

"I have bad news that the team needs to be aware of right away." Jake looked to the side at something out of camera range, then leaned into the video feed. "We're still at the hotel in town with the U.N. delegation that stayed behind. The situation at Ras Lanuf is being broadcast all over the world and is being picked up by social media. Turkey, Iran, the U.S., and Russia, are all mobilizing their military. Including fighter jets. It's going to get really ugly if we can't resolve this situation ASAP."

"How much time do we have?" Augie's mind was racing. With all of those military superpowers involved, this could be the start of World War III.

"A couple hours, max." Jake shook his head. "The only thing holding anyone back from just sending a missile into that warehouse right now is that the two recognized leaders of Libya are in there, and we obviously have some boots on the ground with Nate's capture. And, of course, the U.N. envoy sitting right next to the Prime Minister. No one wants to see all those names on a casualty list."

"So, if we can't resolve this before any fighter jets are deployed, are they going to bomb the warehouse?" Augie bit his thumbnail. That couldn't happen. Almost all the people he cared about in the world were in there.

"There's no telling what could happen. Most of those countries have been backing either Saleh or al-Masli, and maybe a few might be thinking they wouldn't necessarily mind losing them as collateral damage if Atwah was killed in the raid. He has a lot of enemies and if he manages to get his hands on Libya and set himself up as a leader? No one wants that." Jake let out a breath. "I wish I had better news, but whatever you guys have planned, you need to execute it now."

"I'll let Colt know." Augie ended the call and immediately got back on comms. "What's your position, team leader?"

"Getting ready to leave the elevator shaft on the second floor," Colt responded.

"Looks like the guards have stopped searching, and are all on the warehouse floor to see the show," Abby reported. "And none of them gave more than a cursory look at the elevator shaft. Lucky for us."

Augie didn't want to put any more pressure on the team, but having all the information was crucial to making good decisions. Colt had reminded him of that right before this mission started. "Jake checked in and this is turning into an international incident. Fighter jets are about to be deployed from several countries, with the potential of starting World War III if we don't end this. Jake thinks we need to move. Fast."

Colt didn't seem fazed by the news. "Copy that. Let's move into position. Abby, you go to the control room and pull the main switch on the circuit breaker. As soon as the lights go out, I'll throw the flash grenade. Rian will grab the phone and disarm the vest, Brenna will take the Prime Minister, I'll grab Atwah, and Malek will get Nate and have the General and the U.N. reps follow you both out of there."

Everyone responded in the affirmative. Colt's instructions were clear, but Augie wished someone was going to be helping Rian take the phone. Atwah wouldn't just hand it over.

"Don't worry, Augie," Rian said, as if she knew what he was thinking. "I'm good."

That phrase brought a smile to his face. How often had they said that to each other in the last few days? "Copy that. Elliot has been working on an exfil plan and he'll be waiting for you at the southwest office. It has a window that you can use to exit, and there will be vehicles waiting."

"All right, let's do this." Abby sounded anxious to get started. Everyone knew her thoughts were on getting medical help for Nate.

With the plan laid out, Augie turned back to what was happening at the 'tribunal.'" Prime Minister al-Masli had joined Atwah and General Saleh, standing in front of the camera. "I will give you safe passage out of Libya if you will swear never to come back," he offered.

Atwah laughed, holding his hand to his middle. "Prime Minister, you should be more worried about where you will go when this is over. And who you might claim as allies. Even now my men are rising up in Tripoli and Sirte. The people are joining my cause because they see the future and it's in my very capable hands."

Augie hoped that wasn't true, and Atwah was just bluffing. If fighting was breaking out, the other countries who were monitoring the situation might look at it as an excuse to deploy their troops here or begin attacks of their own. Libya was an important foothold in the Middle East, and several countries might want to solidify their position there using the current chaos. Any progress Libya had made towards expelling foreigners would be lost if that happened.

Elliot's voice came over the comms. "We're in p-position at the exfil point. R-ready when you are."

"I'm in the control room," Abby answered. "Tell me when."

"Augie, we'll do it on the next pass, when Atwah is closest to Rian. Everyone focus up. Pull down your night vision goggles." The comms went silent after Colt's instructions.

Augie watched Atwah as he stood in front of the Prime Minister. His arms were raised as he shouted into his face. "You're weak! Everyone sees it!"

The Prime Minister didn't reply, just stared openly at him, so Atwah stalked back toward Rian. Augie began the countdown. "Three . . . two . . . one. Now, Abby."

And then everything went dark.

CHAPTER SIXTEEN

R ian had been expecting the lights to go out, but the deafening sound of the flash grenade caught her off guard. She blinked furiously, trying to clear her vision of the disorienting light from the flashbang, so she could see Atwah. He was still there in front of her. Lunging forward, she grabbed for the phone and missed, though she knocked it from his hand. It skidded across the floor and Rian dove for it, but Atwah grabbed her neck, his fingers nearly spanning her jaw from ear-to-ear.

He leaned close, probably wanting to be heard above all the gunfire and yelling going on around them. His voice was more like a hiss and she cringed. "You cannot save yourself. You will die for the shame you have brought on your country."

Without letting her go, he bent down, and his long arm snaked out to snatch up the phone. All he had to do was get far enough away before he punched in a number, and the vests would detonate. Rian wasted no time and slid her knife out from her sleeve. Though it was a standard military knife she'd been given with the

Griffin Force gear, it hefted the same way her own did. She got a firm grip on it then stabbed Atwah in the hand.

He let her go, screaming in pain as the blade penetrated the back of his fingers. She drew it back and he dropped to the floor, the phone hitting the concrete beside him. Sweeping up the phone, Rian started to run, but after only taking two steps, she felt a hand on her ankle, yanking her backwards. She went down hard.

Kicking out, she connected with Atwah's jaw, and he let her go. Stumbling to her feet, she looked back and saw him reaching for his gun. She tried to scramble away, to get out of range, but she heard the gun go off almost at the same moment that white hot pain seared her shoulder.

Falling to her knees, she was barely able to keep hold of the phone in her hand. She crawled forward on her good arm, wanting to get away before another shot came. Glancing behind her, she saw Atwah's arm raised. Making a split-second decision, she grabbed her knife once more and threw it directly at his center mass. Atwah fell backward. Another shadow was instantly at his side, pulling on his arms, keeping him away from her. Was that Colt?

She didn't wait to see. Stumbling to where she thought the hallway was that led to the exfil point, she blinked away the tears and dust and smoke, trying to get her bearings. Omar's face swam through her thoughts. He'd sacrificed his own life for hers. She had to honor that and keep fighting. Her arm was slippery with blood from her shoulder wound, but she kept crawling forward, praying she wasn't too late, that the team would wait for her. That she wouldn't be stuck here a moment longer.

The voice in her ear startled her. She'd forgotten about the earpiece.

"Rian, you've got to get to the southwest office," Augie sounded worried. She wanted to reassure him, but her breath was snatched away in the pain of her entire left side. Her vision was hazy, but she couldn't tell if it was from the flash grenade, the gunfire going on all around her, or her loss of blood.

"Rian," Augie's voice called out to her again.

He seemed so close and she wished he was right beside her. Holding her. Kissing her. She'd found him too late. In the short time she'd known him though, he'd become a refuge where she was finally safe. How she wanted to be with him one more time.

"Augie," she gasped out.

"I'm here," he told her. "You can do this. I know you can."

She moved forward a bit more, encouraged by his words. She *could* do this. She'd survived so many hard things. This was just one more to get through.

"Rian, I know you're hurt, but you have to hurry or you'll miss your window." Augie was trying to stay calm, but she could hear the tension in his tone. They were going to leave without her.

She willed her body to move faster, but it wouldn't obey. "I'm sorry, Augie," she said, tears rising to the surface. "I can't. I am . . . so sorry."

She could hear him calling for backup for her, but his voice seemed far away now. After all they'd been through, it seemed wrong that escape was so close, but she didn't have the strength to get herself to the rendezvous point. She couldn't go any further. Her arm, her neck, everything was on fire with pain. All she wanted to do was lie down and close her eyes.

She hung her head in defeat just as arms came from behind and scooped her up. She stiffened, her instincts telling her to fight, but her father's voice cut through the muddle in her head. "Tell me where to go, Rian. What's the plan?"

"Southwest office," she managed to get out. She was so tired. It was easy to close her eyes, but she forced herself to keep them open.

He started to move down the smoky hallway. Soldiers ran past them, gunfire echoing through the room. Her eyelids were so heavy, her body so cold. She stopped fighting and closed her eyes. When the cellar had been cold like this, Augie had warmed her. She clung to that memory, to how she'd felt in his arms.

"Stay with me, Rian," her father said as he ran, carrying her as if she weighed no more than she had as a girl. "Stay with me. We're almost there."

Her head rested against her father's chest as she fought to stay awake as he'd asked her to do. Augie's voice sounded in her ear, and she pressed against it, wanting to have him close, even if it was only his voice.

But she could hardly understand what he was saying and she had to concentrate hard to make out his words.

"Missile inbound! Everyone get out and get clear," Augie was yelling into the comms. "Get out!"

Her eyes opened wide as the realization of what was about to happen sank in. She tilted her mouth toward her father's ear, hoping he heard her over the pandemonium around them. "Incoming missile. We have to get out."

He picked up his pace, dodging barrels, people, and pipes scattered over the floor that the earlier explosions must have knocked loose. His steps were steady, though, and he was careful not to jar her too much, but the pain still ripped through her side. She couldn't remember the last time she'd been in her father's arms, but she'd been a little girl and much lighter. His breath was starting to come fast as he carried her now, but she knew she couldn't walk to relieve his burden no matter how much she wanted to.

After what felt like an interminably long journey to get down a hallway to an office, they finally made it. Elliot was at the window, motioning for them to hurry. "Come on," he urged.

Her father carried her to the window. "She's wounded."

Elliot's eyes widened just the tiniest fraction and that's when Rian knew her injury looked bad. But they didn't have time to deal with that now.

"I'm a medic. I'll take c-care of her once we're s-safe." He held out his arms and her father carefully handed her to him. "Did you s-see Colt?" Elliot asked her.

She slowly shook her head. "He might have been fighting with Atwah, but it was dark, so I can't be sure."

"Okay." Elliot looked into the office, as if debating whether to go look for Colt or not, but then turned away and spoke into his comm. "Colt, we've g-got to go now. If you can h-hear me, I'm evacuating the wounded. G-get out of the building."

Trying to hold onto Elliot's neck with her good arm, she looked over his shoulder, and saw her father climb out of the window. They all ran across the packed dirt, heading for cars in the distance. Every lurch against Elliot's chest sent stabbing pains through her side, but she wasn't complaining. Though her body felt like it couldn't take one more step, this was her only way out.

"Radio check," Augie said through the comms.

"I'm here," Rian answered. Her voice was barely more than a croak no matter how many times she cleared her throat. The blood seeping through her shirt seemed to be slowing down, though. That had to be a good sign.

Abby, Elliot, and Malek checked in as well. Brenna and Colt did not. Worry curled in her middle. Had they gotten out?

"Team leader?" Augie asked. "Brenna?"

Rian felt sick when no one answered and Augie tried one more time. His anxiety level had to be through the roof. What had he told her he recited when he was stressed? Some math theorem that she'd never heard of. Was he doing that now? She closed her eyes. Thinking of him dulled the pain for a few seconds, so she let the thoughts wash over her. He was so adorably quirky. Seeing him in action had been an eye-opener, though. He was the support crew, the planner of the operations, and part of the team effort, but he stayed behind. He was the one who worried about sending his friends into danger. Hopefully the worst hadn't happened today.

A loud whine sounded overhead, and the warehouse exploded into a large fireball behind them. Elliot was thrown into the air and he did his best to cushion their fall when they hit the hard-packed ground, but it still felt like a thousand knives had been plunged into her shoulder at once. She couldn't bite back a scream of pain.

"Sorry," Elliot said, kneeling over her. "I promise I'll take care of your shoulder as soon as I can. Augie would kill me himself if I let anything happen to you."

"What's wrong?" Augie said quickly into the comms. "What happened?"

"We're okay." Elliot tried to reassure him at the same time he was attempting to shield Rian from the debris raining down on them. "We're heading for the car and coming to you."

Rian's father had crawled over to them, his brown eyes looking down into hers.

"I'm here," was all he said.

How many times had she wished he'd been there for her? And now he was, but it was too late. Her head started to buzz, and the fire raining down on them was fading away. "Rian." Her father was speaking. And maybe Augie was, too, she couldn't tell anymore. "Hey, are you okay?" one of them asked. Her mind couldn't figure out which one.

But she couldn't answer, anyway, and slipped into unconsciousness.

CHAPTER SEVENTEEN

Augie focused all his attention on the monitors in front of him, hoping for a glimpse of Rian and the team. The warehouse fire lit up the sky, and flaming debris was falling down like hail. There was a small chance some of it might reach some of the storage tanks, but Augie hoped not. If those exploded, the oil inside them would burn for weeks and cost Libya billions in lost revenue. So far, there had been no sign of any of the team. Soldiers were running in all directions trying to escape the fire and flames, but there was no way to see any faces. Colt's large frame should be easy to spot, but he hadn't seen anyone that resembled their team leader yet.

All Augie could hope for was that Colt and Brenna had lost their comms, but were still okay, and that Elliot was getting everyone else to the command center. His stomach was still tight with worry. Elliot had said they were fine, but Augie knew Rian was hurt after her confrontation with Atwah. His mind was going to the worst-case scenario, and he had to pull himself back. Worry never did anyone any good, his mom always said. But sometimes that was hard to remember when it was people you cared about in danger.

Augie couldn't sit still anymore, so he stood to pace in front of the table of monitors. The fluorescent light on the ceiling was pulsing, as if working hard to give off the weak amount of light it had inside. The sound seemed to match Augie's heartbeat. He paced some more and went over everything Rian had said to him before she'd gone radio silent. She'd sounded like she was crying when she apologized to him while she'd been trying to get to the exfil point. Had that been her way of saying goodbye? But her voice when she'd said "I'm here" during the radio check had been steady and clear. That had reassured him. He took in a deep breath and tried to calm his thoughts. He just needed to see her for himself and make sure she was okay.

The control room was clear except for him and two guards near the doorway. At the sound of footsteps in the hallway, both guards raised their weapons. Augie moved closer. Was it an enemy? Or Elliot?

It was neither. When Malek walked in, accompanied by the General and the Prime Minister, Augie tried to hide his disappointment. They were covered in dirt and glass, with a few minor cuts on their faces. One of the guards brought the Prime Minister a chair and he sank down into it, as if the weight of the world rested on his shoulders and it was too much to bear. His features and bearing seemed to have aged in the short time he'd been at the oil terminal. Now, exhaustion showed in every crease of his face.

Malek watched him for a moment, as if wanting to make sure he was okay before he walked to Augie's side. "Any word on Atwah?" He folded his arms and angled himself so he could still see the two leaders he'd escorted inside.

"No. We still haven't heard from Colt or Brenna. Everyone else made it out and should be here shortly." Augie glanced at Malek's torn and bloody shirtsleeve. "Are you okay?"

"Fine. It's just a minor wound." He looked down at his ripped clothing, as if just realizing he hadn't come out of the warehouse unscathed. "We were lucky we got out when we did. Thanks for the warning. Do you have any idea whose missile it was?"

"Not yet. I think it might have been Russia, possibly Turkey, but my sources are looking into it." Augie was grateful he'd gotten the intel about the missile when he had. But it had still been too close.

"It could take weeks to figure out how many casualties there are. There wasn't much left of the warehouse." Malek ran a hand over his face and flicked his gaze over to the monitors. "At least it didn't start any chain explosions of the oil tanks or petrochemical side of things."

Augie agreed. "Yeah, we were really lucky to have the fire contained to the one building,"

It had been a very precise hit, which was one of the reasons Russia and Turkey were suspected of the missile launch. But it was only a guess at this stage of the investigation. There were a few other suspects that had the same technology and a reason to want Atwah dead. But who would be so callous as to blow up a building with so many people inside?

Which brought him back to the team members who were still missing. Augie looked behind Malek toward the hallway. Where was Elliot and the others?

Malek put a hand on his shoulder, his gaze following Augie's to the empty hallway. "They'll be here. It's bedlam out there right now. No doubt they're taking every precaution to stay low and out of sight."

"You're right." He just had to be patient.

Augie turned and was about to walk back to his station when he heard Elliot call out. "Hey, got room for a f-few more?"

Quickly changing direction, Augie strode to his side. Rian was in Elliot's arms, her eyes closed. She was so pale, his stomach tightened in fear.

"She's alive," Elliot reassured him, shifting her weight in his arms.

"Rian," he said softly.

She turned her head. "Hey. I guess I could have used your lucky shirt."

He smiled at her attempt to reassure him. She had a knack for that. "Next time I'll lend it to you." Augie backed up a step, wishing they had somewhere comfortable to lay her down, but all they had was his metal chair. "Set her down over here."

Elliot gently put her down in it, but she still winced and let out a small moan.

"What happened?" He grabbed another chair from the wall and set it up beside hers. "How bad is it?"

"She's got a g-gunshot wound and a possible broken clavicle," Elliot told him matter-of-factly. "There's no exit wound, so she'll need surgery, but I think she'll be fine."

Augie barely had time to digest that information when Abby and another man came in carrying Nate between them. Elliot waved them over and moved the last chair in the room to the other side of Rian.

Once Nate was seated, Elliot bent to look him in the eye. "Welcome back. Did you catch a n-nap while we were all working?"

Nate frowned, his brow furrowed, as if he couldn't make sense of what Elliot was saying. "When did we leave London?"

Abby turned worried eyes on Elliot. "He doesn't remember anything about coming to Libya. He's pretty disoriented."

Elliot nodded and examined Nate's head wound. "That's to be expected with a concussion. We'll keep a close eye on him."

The other man who'd helped carry Nate in stood back, wiping at his dust-covered face, his gaze stopping on Rian. "How is she?" he asked, tilting his head in Rian's direction.

Elliot turned his attention back to her. "We need to get her to a hospital as soon as we can to get that bullet out. But I think she'll be fine."

Augie wanted to ask who the man was, but in the moment, being with Rian was all that mattered. He'd get names later on. She was shifting in her chair, trying to get comfortable. "Do you have the phone with you?" he asked.

She lifted up the phone. "Right here."

"Then let's get this vest off of you, shall we?" No one could be comfortable with explosives strapped to their chest. He hated seeing her wearing it, a reminder of what had nearly happened.

She handed him her knife. Augie carefully cut the straps at the sides of the vest, trying not to jostle her injured side. The dust-covered man whose name he didn't know stepped up and they lifted it off of her together.

When it was finally off her shoulders, Rian let out a long breath and leaned her head back against the wall. Malek joined them, tasking one of the guards with the phone and both Rian's and Prime Minister al-Masli's vests.

"I'm glad to see you," Malek said, crouching next to Rian. "But then again, I never had any doubt you'd get out of there. You're one of the bravest people I know."

"Thanks." Rian tried to smile, but it looked more like a grimace. She held her upper arm with her opposite hand, obviously trying to find a way to relieve some of the pressure of her injury.

Now that the vest was off, Augie could see the location of the gunshot wound and the blood seeping through the material Elliot had wrapped around her shoulder. The trail of blood down her body worried him. They could be stuck here for several hours before it would be safe to transport someone to the hospital. He wanted her to be seen right away.

"It looks worse than it is," Elliot said, giving Augie a quick glance. He was using a water bottle and Malek's keffiyeh to clean up Nate's head wound. "We're going to take care of both of them."

Augie bowed his head. Of course, he was worried about Nate, too, but Rian's gunshot wound seemed life-threatening to him. At least Elliot was nearby in case Rian needed him. He'd saved the team's lives more times than he could count and knew what he was doing. Augie trusted him with his life. And Rian's.

The man who hovered over Rian and hadn't allowed himself to be more than two steps away from her since he'd come in, crouched in front of her. Worry was evident in his gaze.

Augie gave him a side glance. "I'm sorry, I don't think I caught your name."

The man turned his head to look at Augie, then extended his hand. "I'm Steven Perron."

"He's my father," Rian said softly, opening her eyes for a moment, but focusing on Augie and not Steven.

Was her voice getting weaker? The thought distracted him for a moment from what she'd said, but when it did, he could hardly keep his jaw from falling open in surprise. "Your father?"

Steven's eyes had widened when he heard her say 'father.' "I wasn't sure if you remembered. You were so young when I went away."

"Yes, I was. A young girl who needed her father." She didn't turn her head to look at him and every muscle in her body seemed tense. This was a lot to take in, even if she hadn't been wounded.

"I'm sure we'll have plenty of time to talk after Rian's injuries are taken care of." Augie gingerly put his arm around her, not wanting to hurt her, and letting her know that she didn't have to talk right now. He would do everything he could to make her comfortable. To protect her. She leaned her head into his shoulder and closed her eyes again.

Steven observed the scene in front of him. His shoulders had slumped, but his voice was still friendly. "I don't think I caught your name," Steven said, watching Augie hold his daughter.

"I'm Augustus Taylor, but everyone calls me Augie. I'm the computer tech for Griffin Force." Augie met his gaze and held it. "You have an amazing daughter."

"I do," Steven murmured. He looked like he wanted to say more, but clamped his jaw together instead. These two definitely had a lot to talk about.

Later, Augie thought.

Augie kissed the top of her head. She was safe now. Elliot had said she was going to be fine, she just needed medical attention and rest. And Augie would make sure she received both.

Augie let his eyes roam over the monitors to his left. Still no sign of Colt and Brenna. But then his comms crackled to life.

"Anyone there?" Brenna asked.

"We're here. What's your location?" Augie asked quickly. "Is Colt with you?"

"Yes. We have Atwah and we're trying to come in, but a few of his guards spotted us. We could use some backup." Her breaths came in puffs, as if she was running. "Now. We're about half a mile from the warehouse, coming your direction."

Elliot immediately stood. "I'll be right there. Are you in a vehicle or on foot?"

"On foot and carrying Atwah between us. He's a lot heavier than he looks," Brenna grumbled.

"I'll go with you." Malek stepped forward. "And I'm sure the General's men would be happy to help." Elliot nodded and they headed for the exit. Malek spoke briefly to the General on their way out and all three men left. Augie listened on comms as they figured out the best place to meet up with Colt and Brenna.

"We'll need you, Elliot," Brenna said, her voice still strained from the effort of evading Atwah's soldiers and carrying him. She sounded exhausted. "Atwah and Colt are both wounded."

Anger and worry rushed through Augie when she said that, as well as relief. Everyone was alive. Wounded, but alive. That was the good news. Atwah had caused so much suffering, not only for them, but for countless other innocent people, and he was in custody now. It was over. They'd done it. He bowed his head and tightened his hold on Rian.

They sat there quietly, the air in the command center charged with anticipation as they waited for Elliot, Malek and the General's men to bring in Colt, Brenna, and Atwah. When they all finally came through the door, Elliot and Colt were carrying Atwah. Since there was nowhere else, they laid him on the floor. Elliot was completely focused on the man in front of him. Blood covered the front of Atwah's shirt and his leg.

"We've got to get some pressure on this," Elliot said to no one in particular. "Do we have anything that we could use for a bandage?"

The Prime Minister stood and slowly made his way over to the circle of people surrounding Atwah. He wordlessly handed over his keffiyeh. Elliot stared at it for a moment. This keffiyeh was one the Prime Minister had worn for years and was a signature piece of his clothing, said to have been handed down for generations in his family. For him to offer it to the man that had nearly killed him an hour ago was a profound moment to witness.

"Thank you," Elliot said as he took the offered keffiyeh, then bowed his head and went to work, trying to stop the bleeding.

Atwah was in bad shape, though, and from the look on Elliot's face it was going to be touch and go.

He needs a hospital immediately if he's going to survive, Augie thought. But that wasn't possible at the moment.

Malek walked over to the group of men surrounding Atwah. "The General has just apprised me that a perimeter has been set up, and no one is getting in or out of this building, but we are also keeping Atwah's whereabouts to those of us in this room and the General himself. That missile was meant to kill Atwah, so we don't want to advertise his location, but we want him secure."

Colt nodded, but Augie noticed he didn't look at Malek. He couldn't take his eyes off Atwah. "Keep me informed of any developments," was all he said.

Brenna pressed into his side. "We need to get your leg looked at."

"I'm fine," he told her, his normally gruff voice softening for her. "I just twisted my knee when we were running. It's nothing."

That was a relief. Augie watched all his friends, gratitude washing over him that they were all in one piece. He glanced at Atwah on the floor, his breaths coming fast and uneven, but Augie didn't feel anything. He was just glad it was over. They had Atwah in custody, and he was never going to hurt anyone else again.

"How is he doing, El?" Colt asked, pressing his palm into his eyes. "Is he going to make it?"

"He's got a serious knife wound, his l-leg is broken in several places, and he's got some b-burns from the explosion." Elliot's tone was clinical, and his hands flew over Atwah as he spoke. "We need to get him to a hospital, or he won't make it."

"Do what you can. We'll move out as soon as it's safe." Colt moved to Abby and Nate and Augie noticed his limp. Hopefully it was as minor as Colt was making it out to be. They'd definitely have some stories to tell in the after-action report on this operation.

Malek was called to the doorway, where he escorted General Saleh into the room. They conferred quietly for a moment, then both walked over to the Prime Minister and spoke to him. The three men looked stunned. The Prime Minister ran his hand over his face several times, his mouth open. The General shook his head in disbelief. Had something happened? Augie was just about to call Colt's attention to what was happening, but Colt had already noticed.

"What have we got?" Colt asked Malek.

"We've gotten reports that men from the villages and surrounding towns are coming to the gates, chanting their support for General Saleh and Prime Minister al-Masli. They're chanting their names and 'Freedom for Libya.'" Malek's brow creased as his eyebrows drew together. "I can't believe it. They're showing their support."

"I wasn't expecting that," the Prime Minister said, looking over at the general. "Even though it wasn't what we'd planned for today, I'd say the people have spoken. Our efforts for peace and unity in the country are being rewarded. This is wonderful."

"I agree." General Saleh turned to face the Prime Minister head on. "I meant what I said when we were in the warehouse earlier. Working together is best for the country. And I hope the peace process will be ongoing from today."

Prime Minister al-Masli bowed slightly. "I will do all I can to make sure it goes forward, General. We shall work together to find solutions for Libya that will be a benefit to all."

The General bowed as well. "For Libya."

Both men turned nearly in unison to face Augie and Rian. Her eyes were open, staring at the ceiling. She was so still in his arms, but from her uneven breaths, that could be how she was coping with the pain.

"I want to thank you for your bravery, young lady," Prime Minister al-Masli said, dipping his chin in her direction. "You saved my life and put yourself in great danger."

She slowly turned her head so she could look at them. She swallowed and cleared her throat. "You're welcome, sir."

The General spoke up to add his praise. "Yes, you are to be commended for your quick thinking." He stroked his beard, his expression soft. "And even though you were willing to sacrifice everything, I wouldn't want to see you hurt. It may be too dangerous for you to remain in Libya now that your secret is known and has been broadcast so publicly. There are those that would not understand your actions and could use it as a weapon against you. Try to hurt you."

Rian tensed in Augie's arms, her eyes going wide. "That may be true, but I don't have anywhere else to go, sir. Libya is the only home I've ever known."

Her father stepped up to her side and looked between her and the General. "Rian, I know you don't know me very well, but I'd like the chance to remedy that. You can come back to the United States with me." She didn't respond and he rushed on. "But, if you're not comfortable with that, your grandfather is living in Tunisia. I know he'd love to see you again. I could take you to him."

Rian closed her eyes again and tears slipped down her cheeks. "Grandpapa is alive?"

"Yes. We have a lot to catch up on, my dear." Her father took her hand. "But let's talk about that later. Just know you *do* have somewhere to go."

Malek spoke up. "We also wanted to let you know that the last of Atwah's men are being rounded up now. We are still looking for Fahad, his first lieutenant, but he could have been killed in the explosion, and we won't know more details until daylight. But you don't have to wait to get your wounded evacuated any longer. We've cleared a way for you to get to the hospital in Ras Lanuf. Your transportation is waiting outside."

"Thank you, Malek, for all your help. I know you were leery of us at first, but you really came through." Colt shook his hand. "I won't forget this."

"It was an honor to fight beside you." Malek bowed.

Colt turned to the team, a little worse for wear, but still breathing. "Great work, everyone. We've done what we came here to do. Let's get patched up and get some rest."

Nate tried to stand and Abby tucked herself under his arm to steady him. Colt and Elliot carefully picked up Atwah and started to take him down the hall.

"Time to go," Augie told Rian, tucking a piece of hair behind her ear.

She stirred against him, her voice tight with the pain she was obviously trying to endure. "I'm glad you're here."

He held her close for a moment longer. Hearing Colt say it was time to get some rest was the best thing he'd heard all day. He was ready for some R&R and to have the opportunity to spend some time with Rian. He wanted to get to know her without the threat of death hanging over them. And he was grateful he had the chance.

He gently tilted her chin up and gave her a quick kiss on the lips. "Me, too. I didn't want to miss our next game of What's the Weirdest. I've got a good question for you."

"Oh yeah?" she asked, biting her lip as they stood up. "What's that?"

"What's the weirdest thing you've ever seen on TV?" He kept his arm around her, trying to support her as she slowly made her way to the door. Should he try to carry her?

"Hmm…well, today I saw a terrorist hold a tribunal in front of a TV camera. That was pretty weird." She grimaced and clamped her teeth together.

Augie lifted her up in his arms. "That's what I thought you'd say. And I don't think I can top that."

She pressed her lips together and tried to hold onto his neck with her good arm. "So, I win?"

"Yeah. That's two wins in a row now." He made it to the broken front entryway and carried her through. "You're really good at this game."

"I'm just lucky, I guess." She quickly sucked in a breath as he stepped over some broken concrete and jostled her arm.

"Actually, I'm the lucky one." He made it to the car and set her down. "Lucky that I met you."

She sat down in the back passenger seat of the car and he went around to the other side to sit next to her. As Elliot drove them through the gate and away from Ras Lanuf, his mind flashed back to when he'd arrived just hours ago. They were both lucky to have survived. And he'd never forget it.

CHAPTER EIGHTEEN

Rian opened her eyes to sunlight streaming through some sheer white curtains. She was nestled in the most comfortable bed she'd ever slept in. The pillow was so soft and the mattress cradled her just right. She never wanted to leave.

She tried to stretch, but as soon as she moved, the pain in her side reminded her of what had happened last night. When they'd arrived at the small hospital in Ras Lanuf, the doctor had whisked her back to the surgery room and given her a small dose of IV anesthesia that was only effective for the time it took to dig out the bullet. Then her collarbone had been set, and she'd been given a brace to hold it in place. Augie and her father had helped her to the car as the rest of the team waited to see if Atwah would live. Rian just wanted to lie down and sleep for a week.

Her father had a suite at the hotel where he'd stayed with the rest of the U.N. delegation who had been in town for the ceremony between General Saleh and Prime Minister al-Masli. He'd offered to let her stay there to recuperate, and she'd accepted. It was strange to hear his voice and look into his face and think of him as her father, but a little part of her was starting to get used to it.

She moved very slowly so as to not jostle her injured shoulder and finally made it out of bed. There was a small bathroom just off the sleeping area and she walked in there. Her clothing had been so stained and torn, her father had given her one of his t-shirts to wear and a pair of his sweats. It felt normal to wear baggy clothes, but now that her secret was out, she would have a lot more choices. Not today, though. Glad that the elastic at the bottom of each leg on the large sweats kept the material from dragging on the floor, she rolled them up one more time. Carefully washing her face with her good arm, she pulled her shirt collar down to look at her shoulder. The white bandage where the bullet had entered was actually quite small. And the brace she was wearing to keep her shoulder stabilized wasn't as bad as she'd thought it would be. All in all, she'd been very lucky last night.

Once she was as presentable as she was going to be, she used her good arm and made her bed before she walked out. A table was set up near the window and Augie sat there expectantly, as if he'd been waiting for her. Which he probably had. He stood when she appeared and walked to her side.

"Good morning." He glanced at the clock on the shelf. "Or good afternoon. How are you feeling?"

"Like it's time to take another pain pill." She grimaced a bit. The pain was bearable for now, but she never wanted it to get to the level it had been last night.

Augie led her to a chair at the table. "I ordered some room service. Your pills are right by your juice glass."

She looked at the breakfast laid out before her. Bureeks, asida, fruit, and eggs. All traditional Libyan dishes that she loved. They looked and smelled wonderful. "Remember the last time we ate breakfast together?"

"You looked so mad when I handed you a *bureek*. Constantly reminding me to treat you like a young man." His eyes twinkled as he *tsked*. "I'm so glad I don't have to do that anymore. It was hard to remember."

"I could tell." She smiled and picked up a turnover. "How did you sleep?"

"Like I hadn't slept in days. I don't even remember taking my shoes off I was so tired." He stabbed a piece of fruit with his fork. "I was worried you wouldn't be able to sleep with your shoulder brace."

"The pain pill helped a lot." She took a drink of mango juice, savoring the taste. "Where is my father?"

Augie looked at the door at the other end of the suite. "He's on a phone call arranging for a plane to take us and Atwah to the Netherlands. It sounds like they want to turn Atwah over to the International Criminal Court so he can be tried for war crimes at the Hague. Which is what he deserves."

"They'll need some heavy security. Atwah has escaped from every prison he's ever been in." Rian had only taken a few bites of her food, but was already starting to feel full. It seemed a shame not to finish, but she didn't want to push her body's limits right now when she was still recovering.

"I'm sure they're looking into all their options." Augie sipped his drink, but didn't take his eyes off her. "So, will you be going to the States with your father then?"

Rian's stomach fluttered a bit at the question. Was he asking because he was going back to the States as well? Would he want to see her? "I'm not sure. We haven't discussed it. What are your plans?"

They were dancing around what they really wanted to say, but she couldn't very well ask if he wanted to see her again, could she? That seemed too forward, but she wasn't sure. She'd never been in this position before.

"We'll have some downtime now that Atwah is in custody. Between missions, I always try to go back to Virginia and see my mom. Maybe you could visit me there?" He finished his turnover and looked across the table at her. He seemed so confident, but his hands twisting in his lap gave his nervousness away. What was he thinking? Did he not think she would want to see him?

"I'd love to meet your mom," she said. But even as she said the words, the fluttering in her stomach turned to lead. What would his mother think of him bringing home a Libyan girl who'd lived her life as a boy? What if she didn't like Rian?

He watched her face then stood and came around the table. Kneeling in front of her, he took her hand in his. "Rian, I have to tell you something. You . . . well, you mean so much to me. I can see from the look on your face that you're nervous about meeting my mom. But she would love you." He ran his thumb over the back of her hand. "I've never brought anyone over before. I just . . . well, when I was younger, I didn't have time for dating and girls weren't interested in someone who talked about computer codes and math. After I joined Griffin Force, I didn't have time to date anyone. But now that I've met you, I'd like to try and figure things out. I want to get to know you and laugh with you and celebrate that we didn't die yesterday by seeing where this relationship could go."

She touched her palm to his jaw. He was so earnest and her heart melted a little. Moving her hand through his red hair, which was as fascinating to her as he was, she bent down and pressed her lips to his. He cupped her face and kissed her back so tenderly it nearly brought tears to her eyes. He was the perfect man for her.

He stood and gently pulled her up with him without breaking

their kiss or hurting her shoulder. He drew her closer into his embrace with one arm, giving her the same sense of safety she'd felt with him in the cellar. He deepened the kiss, letting his hands roam through her short hair and then skimming down her back. Being with him like this was nearly the opposite of when they'd kissed while being held prisoner in a dark cellar. Now they were standing in the bright sunlight and enjoying their freedom. It was exhilarating.

The door at the end of the room opened, and they quickly broke apart. Her dad walked into the room, a knowing smile on his face. He didn't say anything about them kissing, though, just joined them at the table. "I'm glad to see you awake. How are you feeling?"

He looked between them, and Rian blushed. "Much better, thank you," she said, biting her lip, trying to hold back her smile.

They all sat down, with her father on her right and Augie across the table from her. It was a cozy scene, one she couldn't have imagined happening even a few days ago. She drank the rest of her juice and gave Augie a conspiratorial smile. He grinned back at her, enjoying their not-so-secret secret. It was obvious her father knew what they'd been doing before he arrived at the table. Her blush deepened when she thought of Augie's kiss and how his touch made her feel. Was this how love felt? Could she be falling in love with someone so quickly?

"How did your phone call go?" Augie asked her dad. He was finished with his meal as well, but slowly sipped his drink while her father ate his food.

"Great. The plane is scheduled to land at the Ras Lanuf airport late this afternoon. We'll be flying to Tunis, where Rian and I will get off and surprise her grandfather." He smiled at her. Her heart was light at the thought of seeing her grandfather again after so many years of believing he was dead. But the thought of the flight ahead was bittersweet as well. She'd be getting off the plane in Tunisia and reuniting with her grandfather, but Augie would be continuing on without her.

Her father reached out and patted her hand, but spoke to Augie. "The rest of you will continue on to Amsterdam. Atwah won't be well enough for his trial for several weeks. Once he is able to proceed, Rian and I will meet you there."

That was the one bright spot then. At least they'd be able to see each other again sooner rather than later.

"Oh, and I spoke to Captain Mitchell and got an update while you were both sleeping. Nate has a nasty concussion, but he'll be fine with a lot of rest. Atwah wasn't so lucky. His knife wound caused some internal bleeding, and he had to have emergency surgery to stabilize him. Elliot will be monitoring him on the flight to the Netherlands and one of the nurses from the hospital has also agreed to go." Her father took her fingers and squeezed them in his hand. "Your knife-throwing was accurate and probably saved your life. Some quick-thinking on your part."

She had no doubt that Atwah would have shot her again if she hadn't thrown her knife. "I've had some practice with protecting myself."

Her father grimaced. "I know you were on the streets, posing as a boy. I can't tell you how sorry I am that I didn't find you before that happened. But I swear to you I never stopped looking. I even took this post as the envoy to Libya so I could continue my search. And then when I heard you had been killed along with your mother and grandmother . . ." He closed his eyes for a moment. "I felt like my life was over."

Augie broke in. "Maybe I should give you two some privacy to discuss this."

But Rian reached for his hand. "Please stay." Her heart twisted at the obvious pain on her father's face. "I felt like my life was over, too. I was essentially an orphan with no options." That was such a difficult time in her life. "Soldiers had come to the university and taken Grandpapa. We couldn't understand why they'd target him. He was an economics professor, not a politician. From what witnesses said, he was loaded on a bus with several other professors, and we never saw them again." She wiped a tear that had escaped down her cheek. "We did our best after he was gone, but it was so hard. The revolution changed everything in Benghazi."

"The beginning of the revolution was what made it so challenging for me to find you." He closed his eyes. "I'd been forced to leave in a mandatory evacuation. I'd begged to stay, to bring you and your mother with me, but I was told Americans were being targeted and an attack was imminent. I could send for you once I was safe, they said, but then the revolution made that nearly impossible. I had some sources that occasionally came across information about you and your mother. That's how I found your grandfather. He was being held as a political prisoner in Tripoli. I got him out of there and relocated to Tunisia. But he had no news of you or your mom."

He squeezed her hand again. "Then I heard about the bombings in Benghazi and saw your names on the list of victims." Tears filled his eyes. "You were my family, and you were gone."

The anger and abandonment she'd felt was starting to disappear the more they talked. "Did you never marry again?" She wanted to know what his life had been like since then. What his life was like now.

"No. I wanted to honor your memory by helping the peace process in Libya. That's what I've dedicated my life to." He leaned in. "Rian, I've been given a second chance with you, and I don't want to waste it. I know we have to get to know each other again, but I just want to say that I love you. I've always loved you, and I always will."

Her tears flowed freely now, and she wasn't ashamed. He hadn't abandoned her like she'd thought. He'd looked for her. Loved her. She hadn't felt so light since she'd been a little girl. "I don't want to waste our second chance, either." She squeezed his hand back. To have this much happiness seemed like a just reward after enduring so much suffering. She had her father back. She had a man beside her that she could easily fall in love with, if she hadn't already. And though she wouldn't be able to continue to fight for Libya's freedom in the way she always had, she still had the opportunity to help shape the country's future at her father's side.

"I already told some of my colleagues about your history and fighting with Malek and the General on the front lines. They're excited to work with you as a consultant." He picked up a napkin and wiped away his tears. "I have to admit, I never thought I'd have the opportunity to work side by side with you."

"I didn't, either." She sat back in her chair, soaking up the moment. She was going to remember this day for the rest of her life.

"One of the women in our delegation is about your size and she said she could lend you some clothes until we have a chance to go shopping. I was going to go pick them up. I'll be right back." He stood, but leaned in and kissed her cheek.

Augie waited until her father left, then took her hand and led her to the couch. They sat down, and he put his arm around her, ever vigilant of her sore arm. "I know I've already asked this once, but how are you feeling?" His hand played with her hair, sending shivers down her spine.

"I feel . . . happy." She leaned her head on his shoulder. "Content. Like everything has finally fallen into place." She turned to look up at him. "And you're a part of that, too. I hope you know that."

He moved closer and briefly touched his lips to hers. "I need to thank Malek for sending you with me on that observe-and-report operation."

"Maybe it was your lucky shirt that did it after all," she said with a chuckle, looking over at the plain black t-shirt he now wore.

"You know, since my shirt got ruined, we might have to figure something else out as our lucky talisman." He tucked her closer into his side. "Especially since we probably used up all our luck on this last mission. We're going to need to replenish the magic somehow."

"I think just being together is magic enough." She closed her eyes, listening to his heartbeat under her ear. Life was hard and there were challenges ahead, but she had a family now. She had Augie. And she couldn't wait to see what the future held for them.

CHAPTER NINETEEN

Augie stood on the edge of the tarmac waiting for the plane to land that would take them to Tunisia and then on to the Netherlands. Rian was holding his hand and looking a lot less pale than she had last night. Their breakfast together had cemented his feelings for her. She was everything he'd ever dreamed of---smart, beautiful, brave, and loyal. And while everything was up in the air with their professional lives, personally, they had already figured out how to keep in touch while they were apart until she joined Griffin Force in the Netherlands. He squeezed her fingers and she turned her face up to his with a smile. That was the image he wanted to carry with him every moment they were apart.

Her father was a step in front of him and Rian, his eyes trained on his daughter. He seemed to be as happy as she was about their reunion, as well as supportive of her relationship with Augie. That was a relief. Though, watching Rian and her dad get to know each other again made him want to call his mom and catch up with her.

Steven looked at his watch. "The plane is running a bit late."

"I'm just glad we got a flight out that could accommodate a medical patient." Augie looked over at where Colt, Brenna, Elliot and the nurse were standing. Atwah was on the gurney next to them hooked up to several monitors. His skin had a gray pallor to it, and his bandages covered a large swath of his body. Hopefully he stayed alive long enough to pay for his crimes.

Rian looked at the horizon. "I've never left Libya before," she said softly.

"You're leaving part of your heart behind in Libya." He understood how hard this was going to be for her. "But it won't be the last time you see it."

"I know." She squared her shoulders. He knew that no matter what was in front of her, she'd face it head on. That was just how she was. But if she'd have him, he'd be with her every step of the way.

Nate and Abby stood next to him and Nate looked a lot better than he had the night before, too. "Any more information on that missile attack last night?" Nate asked, turning to face Augie.

"No one's taken credit for it. All the signs are pointing to Russia, but it still could be Turkey. We don't have any concrete evidence yet." Augie adjusted his laptop bag on his shoulder. For once, he wasn't anxious to open his computer. He just wanted to be in this moment with Rian and the team.

"We're just glad everyone made it out of there in relatively one piece," Jake added, as he joined the group with Mya at his side.

"We were pretty worried," Mya added, stepping in front of Jake. She put her hands in her pockets and turned to Augie. "We stopped by to see you and Rian last night, but her father said you'd gone to bed as soon as the hospital released you."

Jake clapped Augie on the shoulder. "Good thing you two got some rest after all you went through this week." He drew Augie into a one-armed hug. "You did great out in the field, but definitely cut a few things too close. I can't imagine the team without you, man, and I don't ever want to find out."

Augie warmed at Jake's words. "Thanks. But I think that was my first and last mission out in the field, so you don't have to worry."

Several soldiers were posted on the perimeter of the runway, wiping away the sweat on their foreheads and using their keffiyehs to shield them from the sun and dust. They looked bored waiting for the plane to get there, but General Saleh wasn't taking any chances. He wanted to make sure Atwah was safely on board that plane and headed toward a real tribunal this time, one that would mete out justice.

The General had wanted to come to see them off today, but he was overseeing the cleanup at the oil terminal and combing through the wreckage of the warehouse. Officials were also counting the dead. Several of Atwah's key people, like Fahad, were still missing, which was a bit worrisome. If he'd survived the warehouse bombing, Augie had no doubt he'd turn up again. While he was happy the situation seemed under control, Augie was glad to be leaving that all behind.

Finally, they heard the plane overhead, and everyone turned to watch it land. When it had come to a stop, two of the soldiers walked forward to meet it. The team did the same. This one was a bit larger than the plane they'd flown to Libya in, and Augie was glad for that. It was also configured a little bit differently to make room for the medical equipment that Atwah would need.

They stood back and watched as the larger than normal door opened and the flight attendant motioned Elliot, the nurse, and the gurney forward. The guards stood sentinel while the gurney was pushed onto a ramp to get it on board. Halfway up, however, the gurney seemed to stick as though one of the wheels had twisted or broken. The nurse was pulling with all her might, and Elliot was pushing, but it just wasn't budging. One of the guards stepped up to help add his strength. Finally, they all disappeared onto the plane.

After several minutes, the rest of the Griffin Force team was still standing on the tarmac waiting to board. Augie assumed the flight attendant would come back to tell them when it was their turn to get on the plane, but she didn't. Maybe it was taking longer than they thought to get Atwah settled. Or maybe there had been a medical emergency?

"What's going on?" Colt murmured. He started toward the plane when the flight attendant appeared in the doorway, the soldier next to her. But it was the look of stark fear on her face that stopped everyone cold. And that's when they all saw it. The gun rammed into the flight attendant's side.

"Close the doors," he ordered her. She bent to obey and Colt took a few steps forward. The soldier turned and pointed his gun at Colt's chest. "Stay where you are. I don't mind shooting you," he said, the keffiyeh on his head slipping down around his neck.

Augie sucked in a breath and felt Rian tense beside him. Fahad. How had he escaped last night and kept himself hidden among the soldiers? But that question was answered when six more soldiers who had been posted at the tarmac surrounded them, guns drawn. Everyone on the team raised their hands. They were outgunned and outnumbered. There was nothing they could do.

The soldiers backed up, keeping their guns on Griffin Force while moving toward the plane. How had traitors infiltrated the General's ranks? Not that it mattered now. Someone had betrayed them all.

The six guards moved up the ramp and helped finish securing the door. Before it was completely closed Fahad grabbed the flight attendant roughly by the arm and threw her the few feet from the doorway to the ground.

And then the door shut with a thud.

The flight attendant picked herself up and limped toward Colt, sobbing. He gently took her by the arms to steady her and she looked up into his face. "He said to tell you that if he finds out you've tracked him or attempted to intercept the flight in any way, he'll kill your doctor friend and the nurse and make sure you get them back piece by piece."

Everyone on Griffin Force stood there in stunned silence and watched the plane rumble down the runway and take off. Augie clenched his fist. How had this happened? Atwah was getting away again, and all they could do was stand there helplessly and watch.

The plane hadn't even cleared the airport's airspace before Colt was striding across the tarmac. "Come on. We've got to figure out where they're going."

Brenna stayed behind to help the flight attendant. Augie turned to follow Colt, keeping Rian's hand in his, the computer bag banging against his other hip as they walked. "Get me an internet connection, and I can get on it, boss."

"We're going back to the hotel. We'll figure out the next step from there." Colt turned to the team. "We're going to get Elliot back in one piece and make sure this is the last time Atwah ever slips through our fingers again. The very last time." His words were clipped. Not angry, just determined. He met every one of their eyes, his promise hanging in the air. Everyone nodded, acknowledging the job in front of them, and that they would work the problem as a team.

"Looks like we're not leaving Libya quite yet," Augie said softly to Rian. "And we could use your help."

"We do make a good team. And I have some contacts in Benghazi that might be able to help us. Especially since two of those soldiers were Omar's men. Maybe they mentioned their plans to someone before they left." She kept pace with him as they continued walking across the airfield.

"Think you can get a meeting with them?" he asked as Nate, Abby, Jake and Mya fell into step beside them.

She raised her eyebrows. "That's like asking if you know Abel's binomial theorem."

He grinned. "How silly of me to question your skills and sources."

Her father joined them on Rian's other side. "Just tell me what I need to do. I have some resources of my own and contacts in the U.N."

Augie looked around him as they reached the airport terminal. They were a team. They could do this. There was no doubt in his mind.

"Just hang on, Elliot," he murmured. "We're coming."

Julie Coulter Bellon is an award-winning author of over two dozen published books. Her book All Fall Down won the RONE award for Best Suspense, Pocket Full of Posies won a RONE Honorable Mention for Best Suspense and The Captain was a RONE award finalist for Best Suspense and Best Audio Book. Most recently her books, The Capture and Second Look were both Whitney finalists for Best Suspense/Mystery.

Julie loves to travel and her favorite cities she's visited so far are probably Athens, Paris, Ottawa, and London. In her free time, she loves to read, write, teach, watch Hawaii Five-O reruns, and eat Canadian chocolate. Not necessarily in that order.

If you'd like to be the first to hear about Julie's new projects and receive a free book, you can sign up to be part of her VIP group on her website www.juliebellon.com

facebook.com/AuthorJulieCoulterBellon
twitter.com/juliebellon
instagram.com/AuthorJulieCoulterBellon